W9-BMM-204

"How do you see me?"

Jeff swished a carrot into the pepper dip and tasted it. "Spicy and delicious," he murmured. He was pretty sure he was playing with fire. Ask him if he cared.

For months—years—he'd been cautious about involvement. Suddenly he wanted closeness… intimacy…touching…

"Don't," Caileen said hoarsely.

"Don't what?"

"Look at me like I'm Red Riding Hood and you're the wolf."

Her husky laughter was shaky, and he was pretty sure she knew exactly what he was thinking. He took a long drink of sangria. It didn't cool his fevered thoughts one degree.

"That's what I feel," he admitted, then laughed again. If he could joke about it, he could control the impulse.

Maybe.

When she looked directly into his eyes, he was pretty sure he couldn't….

Dear Reader,

My family jokes that they can always tell where I've been because my next books are located there. Okay, I confess—I went to the Grand Canyon last year, also Monument Valley, Four Corners, Mesa Verde, Chaco Canyon and the high desert region. My husband, two grandsons, Shasta, our dog, and I camped along the way, sleeping in a tent and cooking over a campfire, feeling like real pioneers. When I wrote the Seven Devils series I knew I had to do the stories of the three runaways in Trevor and Lyric's book. The stories of those orphans, all grown up, the wounded vet who took them in (and whose heart is as big as the western sky) and the awesome landscape of our western deserts came together for me during that trip.

Best,

Laurie Paige

SECOND-TIME LUCKY

LAURIE PAIGE

Huntington City Township
Public Library
255 West Park Drive
Huntington, IN 46750
www.huntingtonpub.lib.in.us

Silhouette®
SPECIAL EDITION®
Published by Silhouette Books
America's Publisher of Contemporary Romance

If you purchased this book without a cover you should be aware that this book is stolen property. It was reported as "unsold and destroyed" to the publisher, and neither the author nor the publisher has received any payment for this "stripped book."

ISBN-13: 978-0-373-24770-7
ISBN-10: 0-373-24770-2

SECOND-TIME LUCKY

Copyright © 2006 by Olivia M. Hall

All rights reserved. Except for use in any review, the reproduction or utilization of this work in whole or in part in any form by any electronic, mechanical or other means, now known or hereafter invented, including xerography, photocopying and recording, or in any information storage or retrieval system, is forbidden without the written permission of the editorial office, Silhouette Books, 233 Broadway, New York, NY 10279 U.S.A.

All characters in this book have no existence outside the imagination of the author and have no relation whatsoever to anyone bearing the same name or names. They are not even distantly inspired by any individual known or unknown to the author, and all incidents are pure invention.

This edition published by arrangement with Harlequin Books S.A.

® and TM are trademarks of Harlequin Books S.A., used under license. Trademarks indicated with ® are registered in the United States Patent and Trademark Office, the Canadian Trade Marks Office and in other countries.

Visit Silhouette Books at www.eHarlequin.com

Printed in U.S.A.

Books by Laurie Paige

Silhouette Special Edition

Lover's Choice #170
Man without a Past #755
**Home for a Wild Heart* #828
**A Place for Eagles* #839
**The Way of a Man* #849
**Wild Is the Wind* #887
**A River To Cross* #910
Molly Darling #1021
Live-In Mom #1077
The Ready-Made Family #1114
Husband: Bought and Paid For #1139
A Hero's Homecoming #1178
Warrior's Woman #1193
Father-To-Be #1201
A Family Homecoming #1292
Make Way for Babies! #1317
***Something To Talk About* #1396
***When I See Your Face* #1408
***When I Dream of You* #1419
The Princess Is Pregnant #1459
Her Montana Man #1483
†*Showdown!* #1532
†*The One and Only* #1545
†*Found in Lost Valley* #1560
Romancing the Enemy #1621
†*The Devil You Know* #1641
†*A Kiss in the Moonlight* #1654
†*The Other Side of Paradise* #1708
§*Second-Time Lucky* #1770

Silhouette Books

Montana Mavericks
The Once and Future Wife
Father Found

The Fortunes of Texas
The Baby Pursuit

The Coltons
The Housekeeper's Daughter

Lone Star Country Club
Heartbreaker

Montana Mavericks:
Wed in Whitehorn
Cheyenne Bride
Outlaw Marriage

Under Western Skies
"One Baby To Go Please"

Claiming His Own collection
†"Something To Hide"

*Wild River
**The Windraven Legacy
†Seven Devils
§Canyon Country

LAURIE PAIGE

"One of the nicest things about writing romances is researching locales, careers and ideas. In the interest of authenticity, most writers will try anything…once." Along with her writing adventures, Laurie has been a NASA engineer, a past president of the Romance Writers of America, a mother and a grandmother. She was twice a Romance Writers of America RITA® Award finalist for Best Traditional Romance and has won awards from *Romantic Times BOOKclub* for Best Silhouette Special Edition and Best Silhouette in addition to appearing on the *USA TODAY* bestseller list. Recently resettled in Northern California, Laurie is looking forward to whatever experiences her next novel will send her on.

This book is for Ryan, Kevin and Shasta, three great traveling companions. Thanks for the s'mores when dinner over the campfire turned into a disaster.

Chapter One

Jefferson Aquilon manhandled the crate into place beside the cabinet, took a deep breath and wondered, for the hundredth time in the past hour, if he was doing the right thing.

Actually, it was a bit late to be thinking like that. Everything he owned had been moved—lock, stock, barrels and sculptures—from Boise to this small ranch near the county seat of Council, Idaho. All his hopes and plans hinged on making it in this new place.

Worry hit him like a sluice of icy water from a mountain spring. He'd made the move for the orphans in his care. Eighteen-year-old Jeremy, who'd taken on a man's responsibility while still a boy, was his nephew. Thirteen-year-old Tony, who'd almost forgotten how to laugh, and Krista, who was ten going on thirty, weren't blood relatives, but they were his second brother's stepchildren, and Jeff was their only surviving relative.

Both his brothers had died young. Lincoln, father of Jeremy and the oldest of the three Aquilon boys, had had a heart attack at thirty-nine. That had been a shocker.

Six months before that, Washington, the middle son, had rolled his truck on an icy road one night and was dead by the time he was found and brought to the hospital. He'd married Tony's and Krista's mom when the kids were still toddlers. Although no adoption records had been found, the two children had taken his last name.

Jeff grimaced. Around the same time, he'd lost his left foot to a land mine while on a tour of duty in Afghanistan.

Life had continued to hand the Aquilons a raw deal. Nearly two years ago, the do-gooders at the Family Services Agency had taken the younger children away from him, saying his two-bedroom trailer wasn't big enough, and put them in foster care.

The foster father had beaten the children until they'd come to Jeremy for help. The three had run away and hidden in the Lost Valley area until found last fall by the Dalton family, who had a ranch there.

Jeff clenched his hands into fists as anger buzzed through every nerve. He forced himself to relax and unpack the crate of woodworking tools.

Things were working out, he assured himself. While *his* family name may not have been enough to convince the juvenile court judge that the orphans would be fine in his care, the Dalton name had. A First Family of Idaho and all that, they'd come through for him and the kids and for that he was grateful.

Moreover, one of the Dalton wives was manager of a private charitable foundation. She'd convinced the directors to supply the down payment for the modern ranch-style home with a bedroom for each child—as Family Services insisted they must have—and that, along with the money he'd saved while in the army, had enabled the move.

Due to high demand for land in the city, he'd sold his place in Boise for top dollar and bought sixty acres adjoining the highway that led to one of the prime vacation spots in the area. The Daltons had helped pack and load his household goods onto a rented truck. They had also repaired the old barn on the property, making it into a shop for his salvage-and-recycle operation, which earned him a living, and his sculptures, which didn't.

So, here he and his little improvised family were, less than a year after the custody hearing, settling into their new home, the kids enrolled in the local school system and the spring season—it was the last day of March—erupting into daffodils and birdsong.

His heart rate went up while an odd emotion skittered around inside him. He paused while unloading a box of old estate ogees he'd recently purchased and analyzed the feeling. Surprise caused a smile to tug at his lips.

Hope. Anticipation. An expectation that everything, at last, would be right with their world.

And what planet would that paradise be on? the doubting part of him inquired.

Something his mother had once said while she'd hidden him and his two brothers from their father, who'd been in a drunken rage at the time, came to mind.

"Shh," she'd murmured at their whimpers. "Someday you'll grow up and make your own life, one that will be much better than what your father and I have given you."

Going outside to retrieve another box, Jeff squinted into the bright afternoon sunlight while recalling his determination to make a decent life for himself. He'd finished high school and joined the army, becoming a Ranger. However, nothing had turned out quite as planned.

A car turned into the lane leading to his place, interrupting the relentless flow of memories. A woman was at the wheel. Putting aside the lingering worries, he left the workshop and started for the house as the woman parked and headed for the front door.

She stopped on the new sidewalk made of rosy-toned pavers and lined with flowers planted by the kids, surveying the place as if thinking of buying it.

Wariness caused him to pause.

Her attire was all business, but there was something youthful, even graceful about the way she stooped to sniff a particularly aromatic rose.

He assumed she was there on business, probably referred by one of the local building contractors or interior designers who used his salvage services, but for an instant he wished she were there for him.

He frowned at the odd sensation and attributed it to spring fever or whatever had caused the mixed emotions of the morning. "Hello," he called.

She straightened and pivoted toward him. She was older than he'd first thought. Probably around his age, he decided as he came closer, noting the faint lines fanning out from the corners of her eyes.

"You looking for someone?" he asked politely.

She removed her sunglasses and looked at him. Her eyes were light green with gold flecks in the center. For a strange second, he felt as if she were gazing into his soul…and wasn't impressed by what she saw.

Caileen Peters glanced at her notebook. "Jefferson Aquilon?" She gazed at the man who approached her with only a hint of a limp. He matched the description given to her.

Except the file hadn't mentioned he was a man straight out of a Brontë novel—dark and brooding, wary and watchful, interesting as only a mature man could be—one who was experienced and confident of his place in the world.

An odd shiver danced over her skin, leaving a trail of goose bumps along her arms and scalp.

Get a grip, she advised, reining in her imagination and concentrating on the business at hand. She raised her eyebrows as the silence spun out between them. In Family Services parlance, this was known as "taking charge."

"You found him," he said, a question in his eyes and no smile of welcome on his angular, attractive face.

He was a bit over six feet, with broad shoulders and a muscular frame. The laugh lines radiating from his eyes nicely balanced the frown line across his forehead.

He had dark hair, a shade between brown and black, and his eyes were so dark they, too, appeared black. Looking into them was like staring at a blank wall. There was a closed aspect to him, as if he didn't allow anyone into his inner thoughts.

He was a year older than her own forty years—forty years!—and a veteran who'd had his foot blown off by a land mine while in Afghanistan. He'd also had some problems with the people at Family Services down in Boise last year, so she hesitated in telling him the purpose of her visit. No one liked to be poked and pried at by strangers.

"You have the advantage," he finally said. "Are you going to tell me who you are?"

She introduced herself and added, "I work for the county. Family Services."

His frown line deepened. "What do you want?"

A new life might be nice. "I've been assigned to this case. Now that you've completed your move," she added when he didn't respond.

"I thought we already had a case worker."

"Not in this county. I've spoken to the counselor in Boise and to Lyric Dalton up here, so I think I have a pretty good idea of your situation."

"Do you now?"

The tone was more than a little cynical, with an undercoating of sarcasm and suspicion. Exactly like most of her clients at the first meeting, only more so.

Her counterpart in Boise, Mrs. Greyling, had been a tired, bitter woman who should have retired before she reached burnout. She'd been instrumental in removing the children from this man's care and had been humiliated when they ran away from the foster home she'd recommended.

Caileen smiled at the man who'd taken the orphans in. That the children had asked to stay with him was in his favor, and Lyric had assured her he was a truly caring person. His present attitude wouldn't influence her impression of him. Only time would do that, and she would have lots of time to get to know him and his family well.

Well, maybe not. She'd turned forty last week. Her daughter had informed her she was middle-aged and didn't understand anything about the younger generation.

"I'm so glad your place here is finished," she said, focusing on the silent man. "The children have settled very well into school and the community, from all reports."

"So you've checked them out and now you've come to do the same with me," he stated.

She held her smile in place. "Yes. I need to see the house, if you don't mind."

"Would it do any good if I did?" His unexpected smile was heavy with irony, but it did nice things for his face.

Not believing in evading the issue, she said, "Not if you want to keep the children."

He took one step and was in her face. "Let's get one thing clear from the beginning. Those kids have been pushed around enough. The judge said they could live with me and this is where they will stay."

"I think that would be best, too," she said in the calmest voice she could muster. She inhaled deeply.

A scent like wild thyme and balsam filled her, along with the clean odor of sweat and soap and aftershave lotion. The pure male aroma did something to her insides, and for a moment, she remembered being young and in love.

She sucked in a harsh breath and brought herself back to the present.

"Are you okay?" he asked, his chocolate eyes narrowing as he studied her.

"Yes. Yes, of course."

Moving on, she mentally made notes on the flowers, the neatly mown grass on each side of the walkway, the rocks used to outline and separate each space. Beyond the small lawn, the ground was mulched or graveled for low maintenance and conservative water use.

From the files, she knew he was a sculptor as well as a salvage expert. Feeling they needed to find neutral ground, she asked, "Did you do those?" and pointed to a birdbath covered in bright ceramic pieces that held two sculptures made of copper wire. One was a bird perched on the edge of the basin and the other was a dog with its front paws on the opposite side while it peered at the bird.

His gaze followed hers, and he nodded.

The pleasing diorama was centered in a circle of river gravel. A wooden bench nestled close by under a copse of silver birch trees. The sky formed a perfect backdrop of blue with a few puffy white clouds to add contrast.

She wondered what it would be like to sit there on a warm summer evening and watch the stars come out.

"If we could go inside?" she suggested, shaking off the spurious notion.

He nodded and led the way to the front door, opening it and gesturing for her to go in first. She stepped into the modest home and stopped abruptly, unprepared for the lovely welcoming decor of the room, the warmth that seemed to reach out and grab her heart.

His hands settled on her shoulders as he came to a halt after almost crashing into her. Through her somber business suit, her skin prickled with awareness of his body so close behind her. She moved forward, away from him and his disturbing masculinity.

"This is charming," she told him sincerely.

His smile returned, a real one. "Krista was in charge of the decorating. She consulted with the Dalton wives."

Caileen ignored a flash of envy for the women he'd mentioned. Years ago, when she'd started on her career, the Dalton case history had been presented to her as a most successful blending of families. This achievement represented the paradigm she was to aspire to in her cases.

The former Dalton orphans were all happily married now, their families integrated into one ideal whole.

However, one needed ideal material to work with in order to perform miracles. She was willing to settle for a functional arrangement. Turning over a page in her notebook, she noted the cleanliness of the home, the comfortable furniture and the evidence of age-appropriate games and books as well as a television.

A vase of golden daffodils adorned the dining table and potted plants filled the kitchen windowsills and various corners of the large, open living area. The walls were painted a soft golden yellow with a sienna glaze that added texture. Other colors—yellow, green and pink—had been chosen to complement the braided oval rug that artfully defined the seating area of the large living room.

A copper sculpture of a mailbox in front of a farmhouse decorated one wall. Charcoal drawings of each of the children hung on another. The drawings were caricatures that were funny and tender at the same time. She noticed the initials on the drawings were the same as his.

"Is that your work?" she asked, realizing his talents were much greater than indicated in the case study folder.

Builders and interior designers depended on him in their remodeling efforts, she'd learned. He bought old furniture, even houses, and reclaimed the useable features such as mantels, lintels, doorknobs and decorative moldings.

While investigating his character, she'd made a point of checking out two of his metal sculptures in Boise, each a featured item in the front yards of very expensive homes. The reports hadn't mentioned his additional artistic abilities, such as the drawings.

"Yes."

The answer was grudgingly given. She didn't write this observation down. "They're quite good. Children need to see pictures of themselves. It gives them a feeling of worth and self-confidence, of being important to others."

When he said nothing, she continued on the tour.

In each of the bedrooms there was a desk and bookcase. Each desk had a dictionary on it. The bookcases were filled with reference books and novels that reflected the personal tastes of the occupants. She noted this with approval.

"Excellent," she said, giving him a nod and closing the notebook when she finished the inspection.

His chest lifted as if he took a deep breath of relief. It was the only sign he'd displayed of being apprehensive about her visit. "The last room is down this way."

She followed him to the opposite side of the house, although there was really no need to see his quarters.

But she was curious.

The bedroom was large and rather narrow. A king-size bed occupied one end. There were tables and lamps handily located on each side of it. An alcove with an easy chair, a rocker and a bookcase invited one to linger and read. A large bathroom was next to that. The color scheme was a soft, smoky blue with touches of tan and mauve.

Envy ran through her like a summer heat wave.

"Your home is lovely," she managed to say. "It will be a wonderful place for children to grow up."

"If the adults make it that way," he said, qualifying her impulsive statement. "Would you like a cup of coffee?"

Her surprise must have showed.

"I want to ask you some questions," he added.

"Coffee would be fine."

Once they were seated at the dining room table,

each with a steaming cup of fresh coffee, he gazed out the window as a nippy March breeze stirred the daffodils.

"How long do you have to check me out before you decide the kids are okay here?"

"Foster children are under the care of the state and county until they're adults."

"Eighteen or twenty-one?"

"Eighteen."

The frown line indented across his forehead. "So you'll be keeping an eye on us for several years."

"Until Krista is eighteen."

"Seven years and one day," he said. "Could they be taken away at any time if you give the word?"

"Not quite as easily as that," she told him. "I would have to be able to show cause."

"What would that be?"

She wondered what he was getting at. "Physical abuse—"

"Like the beatings that made Tony and Krista run away from the other foster home?"

Caileen reached across the table and laid a hand on his arm. "I'm terribly sorry for that. We really do try very hard to prevent such things."

He stared at her hand until she withdrew it, then peered into her eyes. "What else?"

"Mental abuse," she continued. "Alcohol abuse. One of the most common causes for removal in foster families is spending the allowance for the children's food and clothing on personal items."

"That won't be a problem here."

"I didn't think it would. Another thing the courts frown upon is lack of supervision."

"I see." He gazed out the window again. Caileen sipped her coffee, which was surprisingly good, and waited for his next question.

"Was Krista physically abused?" he asked. "Apart from the beatings?"

Caileen shook her head. "No. Why do you ask?"

"She seems afraid of me sometimes. She doesn't like it when both the boys are out at one time."

"That could be separation anxiety," Caileen said after considering the facts. "She depended solely on Jeremy and Tony for her safety during the time they were hiding out. It can be frightening to need another that much, to know that without them, she might have to return to foster care and face the same situation again but alone this time."

"Why wouldn't she come to me? I've never hurt them."

"Perhaps she isn't sure you really want her." Caileen glanced at her watch. She'd been there nearly an hour and still had two other homes to visit. Rising, she gathered her purse and notebook. "I think we should give her time to realize that her life isn't going to suddenly change again."

"She needs to regain her trust in people," he concluded, the cynical note back.

"Yes. Don't rush her. Just be available if she wants to talk. Stories can help children open up. I have some good books that would be right for Krista. I'll see that you get them. You might read a chapter to her each night. Oh, and have her read one to you. That helps enormously with reading skills, we've found."

"Okay. When can I get the books?"

Clearly he wasn't one to waste time. "I'll bring them over tomorrow." She checked her day planner. "Around noon. That's the only time I have free."

"Fine. At noon then."

He strode toward the front door, the interview over as far as he was concerned. She found herself as much amused by his manner as touched by his obvious concern for the orphans in his care.

"Mr. Aquilon—"

"Jeff," he corrected. "Since we're on day one of a seven-year relationship, we may as well be on a first-name basis."

"Jeff," she acknowledged. "I want you to know we're on the same side where the children are concerned."

He looked as if he might dispute that, then he nodded, so solemnly it touched something deep inside her that hadn't been disturbed in a long, long time.

A few minutes later, giving one last wave over her shoulder as he watched her departure, she turned onto the main road and headed for her office.

Her conclusions would be fairly easy to write up. The home was perfectly acceptable. The man was…

She considered several adjectives as she wound her way down the tree-lined country highway. Strong. Cynical. Self-contained. Kind. Caring. Responsible.

If her husband had been like Jefferson Aquilon, maybe they would still be together. Maybe life would have been easier for their daughter if she'd had a father who could have stuck it out during the hard times.

Instead, Brendon, her twenty-six-year-old surfer hero, had run out after five years of married bliss. Not that things had been much fun the last four of those years. With a child had come responsibility. Zia had needed a home, not a van, to live in. She'd needed medical treatment for her asthma.

The family had needed steady income, more than Caileen could provide from her nursing assistant salary while she tried to pursue her degree in counseling. Her parents, furious with her marriage, hadn't offered help before or after the divorce.

Unfortunately, she now knew exactly how they'd felt. Experience was a great teacher. Putting thoughts of the past on hold, she finished her afternoon appointments and went home.

The two-bedroom town house was cold when she let herself inside. Her daughter wouldn't be home for another hour or so due to a late afternoon class. She turned up the thermostat, changed to a pair of old sweats and ate leftovers and a salad for dinner.

Later, over a cup of hot tea, she pondered the visit to the Aquilon place.

Jeff's many talents had surprised her. Obviously he was more than a glorified junk dealer. After the visit, she'd had to revise her opinion of him.

Not that she hadn't been prepared for him to be a nice person. Lyric Dalton had assured her he was. But he was much more than the surface evaluation written up in the case notes by the former counselor.

For one thing, he hadn't mentioned losing his foot in service to his country. He seemed to have adjusted quite well to the prosthesis that had replaced his left foot. Some people would have tried to engage her sympathy on that score, but he hadn't. Although he had a slight limp, he didn't let the disability interfere with his work as far as she could see.

Her impression was that he took life as it came and dealt with each issue head-on. His concern and questions had all been focused on the orphans in his care.

After having the two younger children taken from him for no good reason—in his estimation, at any rate—he had a right to be cynical and distrusting of her department. Most people were.

Welcome to the club, she should have told him.

Her mother and grandmother had been social workers. Like them, she'd gone into it wanting to help families—especially those with children—make it. Lately she'd wondered if the emotional toll was worth it.

She sighed and listened to the wind in the cottonwoods outside the two-family house she'd bought twelve years ago in order to provide a stable home for her daughter. The rent from the other half had paid for braces and the trendy—but pricey—clothing all teenagers thought they couldn't live without.

Her handsome, perfectly built, young husband had left their cozy nest when his daughter was four. Zia had never had a clue about the daily struggle to pay the babysitter, her college tuition and all that was needed to keep body and soul together during the three years that followed. Caileen hadn't wanted her to.

She'd lived in university housing and arranged a babysitting co-op with other student mothers. She'd worked afternoons in the psychology department and weekends as a dishwasher at a restaurant where they'd let her bring her child. She'd found she could survive with a heart that felt as if it had been trampled in the dust and left for dead.

With her master's degree and a job offer from the local Family Services office, she'd moved to Council, bought the two-family home and settled into the hectic routine known as her life.

She hoped, for Jeff Aquilon's sake, he had an easier time rearing his three kids than she was having raising her one. Speaking of which, where *was* Zia?

With Sammy Steele—she answered her own question. Her beautiful, precious child was in love…with a young man who bore all the charming but unreliable traits of her handsome, laughing father.

How could Caileen protect vulnerable, headstrong Zia from the temptation of a boy who promised the moon and stars, but delivered only heartbreak?

Ah, well, a parent could only do so much without alienating her child. Unfortunately, she'd already crossed that nebulous line. She sighed. When she'd been nineteen and madly in love, no one had told her how difficult it was to be a parent.

Not that she would have listened at that age. She mentally winced, realizing her child was as blindly trusting in the future as she'd once been. How did one learn to choose wisely?

She still wasn't sure she knew the answer to that question, so how could she expect nineteen-year-old Zia to do better? After all, *she* was supposed to be the expert on family problems and solutions.

Right. As soon as she found a reliable crystal ball, she'd solve the problems of the world.

Chapter Two

"We passed our first inspection today," Jeff told the other members of his household that evening. "I think."

"Ah, the Family Services witch was here," Jeremy wisely concluded. "Did she arrive on her broomstick?"

Tony and Krista grinned at the eighteen-year-old's insouciant remarks.

Jeff did, too. "Nah, they use cars nowadays. It's part of their disguise. She approved of the house." He directed a glance at Krista. "She especially liked the way it's decorated. I told her you did most of it."

Krista, shy about any kind of praise, blushed and immediately concentrated on her task of setting the table.

When dinner was ready, Jeff paused before taking

his seat. "Tonight we celebrate two special events. First, we pay homage to Anthony, who has reached the distinguished age of fourteen."

Jeremy and Krista cheered and clapped.

"And Krista," Jeff continued, "our own special princess, who will be eleven tomorrow."

Krista had taken a lot of teasing over the years about being an April Fool's baby. She'd asked if she could have her birthday dinner when her brother had his. Tony, good-natured and protective, had okayed the idea.

While Jeff and Tony applauded and offered compliments to Krista, Jeremy brought in the cake Jeff had baked and hidden in the pantry until it was time for it to serve as the centerpiece during the meal.

After eating grilled chicken and roasted vegetables, Jeff and Jeremy lit candles and sang the birthday song. Tony and Krista blew out the candles, then Krista cut the cake.

"Oh, I nearly forgot," Jeff said. His smile belied his words as he removed two boxes from behind the sofa and handed them to the birthday honorees.

Jeremy pretended he couldn't remember where he'd secreted his gifts. He looked behind chairs and in cabinets to no avail.

"In the hall closet," Krista finally told him, somewhat exasperated by his memory loss.

Jeff hid a grin.

Jeremy snapped his fingers. "That's right!"

Krista and Tony rolled their eyes, then smothered

their laughter behind their hands when their foster cousin returned with two packages wrapped in brown paper and tied with string.

"I couldn't find the gift paper," he explained.

"It's stored in your closet," Jeff said.

"Well, no wonder I couldn't find it. I never look in the closet."

That brought more smothered chortles from the younger two. Jeff experienced a return of the odd emotion from earlier in the day, the feeling that they had turned a corner and all would be well with them. If the Family Services people would leave them in peace.

While the kids opened their gifts—a mobile DVD/CD player with headphones from Jeff and three DVDs featuring current music idols from Jeremy for Krista, for Tony, the new sneakers he'd wanted, plus a pedometer to measure his track workouts from Jeremy and books for both of them—Jeff analyzed the visit from Caileen Peters.

Something about her had haunted the remainder of his afternoon. From the moment she'd arrived, he'd noticed things about her.

For instance, she'd liked the flowers he and the kids had planted. She'd been very complimentary of the house and the kids' bedrooms. That had been a relief.

On a different level, he'd noticed the way she moved, the way she'd inhaled the spring air while she'd admired the garden. He'd liked her calm manner and her smile.

And her hair. The way it gleamed with golden highlights in the sun, like sparks from metal when he was welding. The way the breeze had caused the strands to lift and dance over each other. The way she'd brushed it away from her mouth.

Her lips. Soft-looking. Unintentionally kissable.

The fullness of her breasts that the stern business attire hadn't been able to hide.

He hadn't had time to notice a woman in months, maybe years. After a long bout with pain and physical therapy and adjusting to the prosthetic foot, he'd retired from the army with his twenty years in. The pension, plus the disability pay, had helped finance the start of his business.

Next, the three youngsters had moved in with him for six months before the younger two had been taken away. Four months later, all three had disappeared.

The caseworker had given him a lot of grief over that, as if he'd been the one who'd put them in that miserable excuse of a foster home.

That brought his thoughts back to Caileen Peters. At least she didn't seem to be an ogre like the other woman had been. She'd seemed genuine in her concern for the children.

An unexpected stirring in his blood startled him. Man, he must be getting desperate if he was hung up on a damn social worker!

Krista came to him, interrupting the ridiculous ideas running through his head. She kissed him on the cheek in her sweet, shy manner. "Thank you for the present, Uncle Jeff."

"Wow, I must be a prince," he said, clutching his chest. "I just got kissed by a princess."

"Sorry, Uncle," Jeremy wisecracked. "Go look in the mirror. You're still a frog."

Krista scowled. "He is not a frog! He's the most wonderful person in all the world!"

"The princess has spoken," Jeff told his smart-mouth nephew, "and you, Sir Lout, may clean up the dishes."

"The Knights of the Round Table didn't do dishes," Jeremy grumbled, then chuckled as he gathered the used plates. The other two helped.

Jeff crossed his prosthetic foot over his right leg and rubbed his left knee. He was tired from the unusually hard day of unpacking and storing his tools and salvaged treasures, but it was a good kind of tired.

A sense of well-being poured over him like a gentle rain. It didn't get any better than this.

Caileen thought the day couldn't get any worse than it already was. She'd started out on a sour note, arguing with her daughter about a weekend trip with her boyfriend. Then she'd had a flat tire on the way to the office. The judge in juvenile court had spoken sharply to her for not having all the facts on a case she'd just been given two days ago.

Happy April Fool's Day.

She should have stayed in bed and called the

office and told them she was sick. That's what she'd felt like doing every day of late. However, she'd never allowed herself to wallow in self-indulgence, so her attendance record had been perfect over the past five years. Where was her gold star?

Ah, well, one day at a time and don't take anything too seriously. That was her philosophy. Too bad she couldn't live up to its simplicity.

Turning onto the lane leading to the Aquilon place, she frowned at the pleasant homestead, unreasonably irritated by the flowers, the artfully placed benches and copper sculptures dotted around the landscape.

After parking in the shadow of a cedar tree, she sat there for a minute, aware that the appearance of the place was that of an ideal home. She'd once thought with enough hard work on her part she could make life fit a perfect pattern. Events had taught her it couldn't be done.

In spite of her stoic acceptance of reality, she felt a twinge of longing for things to somehow be different and one of sadness because they weren't.

The front door opened and Jeff Aquilon appeared on the rose-bordered deck that served as a porch and defined the entrance to the house. It was warm today and he was dressed in lightweight cargo pants. A tool belt clung to his narrow waist, a hammer dangling from a hoop on it.

Today he looked younger and more relaxed than yesterday. His manner was rather more welcoming.

Had she not known he had a prosthetic foot, she probably couldn't have detected it in the way he moved.

A quizzical glance from him prodded her into remembering why she was here. She picked up the three books, exited the car and went to the porch. "Hello. I remembered the books." She held them out to him, stopping at the limestone slab that served as a step onto the deck.

His hand brushed hers as he accepted the books. Tingles reverberated along her fingers and up her arm. She drew back in shock while alarm bells went off in her mind.

"Lunch is ready," he announced, holding the door open.

She stood there as if rooted to the spot. "I, uh, didn't expect anything. You don't have to feed me."

"You're using your lunch hour to bring the books out. That's a twenty-minute drive each way. The least I can do is offer you a meal. If that's allowed?"

"Well, yes. I mean, of course it is. There's no rule against eating…"

Listening to her flustered statements, she gave a mental groan at how inane she sounded.

"That's a relief to know," he murmured sardonically.

That brought her back to an even keel. She stepped into the house, her senses filling with the spicy scent of his aftershave as she passed him, then with the mouth-watering aroma of a hot meal. The table, she saw, was already set with large bowls on striped placemats. A ceramic casserole was in the center on a polished marble lazy Susan.

"It's beef stew," he said, laying the books on a sideboard and placing the tool belt beside them.

Not at all sure this was wise, she took a seat. "The books are stories of children who have all the cards stacked against them, but they make it anyway," she said, keeping the reason for her visit strictly official.

"Kids like to see how others manage in bad situations, I suppose." He served her from the casserole first and placed a basket of hot fry bread, wrapped in a tea towel, close at hand. A bowl of mixed fruit was at each place.

"This looks wonderful. A well-balanced meal," she told him in approval. "Lots of fruit and vegetables."

His slight smile caused her throat to tighten. "I've read all the articles on nutrition in the paper, so I'm trying to do a good job for the kids. This was to impress you with my skills."

Surprised at the admission, she laughed. "I am impressed, I assure you."

"Good."

He settled in his chair and they ate in silence for a few minutes. Every time she glanced up, her eyes met his. She wondered what he was thinking…if he approved of her soft pink spring outfit…what he expected from a woman in a personal relationship…why no woman had snagged him long ago….

"Everything is delicious. Did you make the fry bread from scratch?" she asked, desperate to divert her thoughts from this strange pattern.

He shook his head. "My mother used to cook it for my brothers and me. She used boxed biscuit mix. She said that was cheating, but she wouldn't tell if we wouldn't. It was our family secret."

"That's a good bonding device."

The dark eyebrows rose in question.

"Having a fun secret to share as a family," she explained. "Your mother had good parenting instincts."

She knew his mother had died several years ago from a rare form of cancer and his father of liver malfunction associated with alcohol when the three boys had been teenagers.

Her own parents, she mused, were alive and well, both now retired and living in Arizona. Her father had been an accountant. They'd never been very close as a family.

She thought of all the times she could have used their help while raising Zia and finishing the work for her counseling degree. But she'd been too proud to ask and they'd been too rigid to volunteer.

Her host's manner seemed introspective as he gazed out the window for a moment. "She loved us. I think she would have given her life to protect us boys."

At his tone she again felt that odd stab of envy, as if his life had been richer than hers. She mentally sighed in disgust with herself. She was so dissatisfied of late.

Was this the fabled midlife crisis?

"I know the feeling," she said, thinking of her daughter and how to pry her away from Sammy Steele.

"How?" he asked. He glanced at her ringless hand. "Do you have children?"

"Yes. A daughter. She's nineteen."

When she didn't add more, he asked, "Is there a father in the picture?"

She nodded stiffly, still feeling the sting of her poor choice in a mate. "We divorced when she was four. I thought we needed a house and steady income. He liked living in a van and surfing the best waves from California to Florida and all beaches between." She shrugged as if it didn't matter.

"Do you ever hear from him?"

"Zia does. He drops by occasionally and sends cards at Christmas and her birthday."

"You sound surprised."

"That he'd remember? I used to be. In some ways, he's actually a good father. He cares for her. In his own way."

"As long as it doesn't interfere with the surfing?"

While his tone was ironic, his smile was real. She smiled, too. "He still surfs, but he owns a construction firm, too. He's been married three times."

"You've never tried it again?"

"No," she said quite forcefully. "Once was enough."

It occurred to her that she'd shared more of herself with this man than with anyone in a long

Huntington City Township
Public Library
255 West Park Drive

time. She clamped her lips together and reminded herself that she was the counselor and he was the patient.

Well, not really, but he was part of the case that was now under her cognizance. She must maintain the proper professional distance.

"Would you like more stew?" he asked.

Staring at her bowl, she realized she'd eaten all of the delicious meal. "No, thank you. Everything was very good. I can't remember when I've had such a treat."

"I hope you saved room for birthday cake. We had a joint celebration for Tony and Krista last night."

The cake was a little lopsided. Crumbs marred the smooth surface of the creamy icing. Four slices were missing, and she could see that it was chocolate inside.

If it had been any more wonderful, she might have burst into tears.

"We prefer chocolate to any other flavor," he said.

"So do I. I may be a chocoholic."

He laughed at that, a rich sound that rolled over her with the sudden pleasure of bells heard in the distance on a Sunday morning in late spring. She could have fallen in love with him for his laugh alone.

After eating the delicious cake, which he admitted he'd made from a mix, she went over the story lines in the books she'd brought and suggested the reading order.

"Strength must come from within," she concluded, "but humans are clan animals. We need others. I think Krista has a good basis in life. She was secure in her mother's love and that of your brother. From the children's accounts, he was a good father to them."

"He didn't like being tied down. As a family, they moved around a lot until his wife grew tired of it and decided to stay in one spot."

"Was that when they divorced?"

"Yes."

"Then both your brothers died."

He nodded. "Within six months of each other and shortly before I stepped on a mine in a field that was supposed to have been cleared. It was sort of freakish—as if the fates were determined to wipe out the whole family."

"Sometimes it seems like that," she murmured. "My records don't indicate a marriage for you."

"No. I got the classic Dear John letter when I was in the army."

"I'm sorry."

His smile was unexpected. "Don't be. Oddly, after I got over the wound to my pride, I realized I didn't really miss her. It was having someone waiting that I missed."

Caileen thought this over. "You didn't love her."

He shrugged. "I suppose not. Not enough for a lasting marriage, I realized later."

"You were wise to recognize it in time," she said.

"Well, she was the one who broke it off. I was merely relieved."

They laughed together. It was the nicest sound.

"I'm going," Zia said in her defiant voice.

"What about the term paper you're supposed to turn in next week?" Caileen asked, keeping her tone level when she really wanted to shout and forbid her daughter to go off for a weekend camping trip with the love of her life.

Zia gave her an irritated grimace. "I hate doing term papers. I should have bought one on the Internet."

Caileen gave a gasp of shock. "That would be cheating."

"Mother, you are such a Puritan."

"Maybe so, but you have a whole summer coming up—"

"That's months away!"

"Two months isn't a lifetime."

"Living here feels like it," Zia grumbled, loud enough to be heard, but soft enough that Caileen could have ignored the statement.

"When you can make it on your own, you're free to do so," she told her daughter, wishing Zia hadn't inherited her stubborn genes.

Zia looked mulish, but said, "I'll just go for tonight and come back in the morning and finish the stupid paper."

"That sounds like a reasonable plan."

Zia flounced down the hall to her room. Caileen ate her dinner and took the plate to the kitchen. Zia had already stowed her used dishes in the dishwasher.

A neat house was one thing Caileen insisted on. Decent grades were another. Money for tuition was too hard to come by to be wasted.

For a second, she wondered if her daughter saw her as unyielding, the way she viewed *her* parents. While she tried to be tolerant and understanding, there was a point within herself that couldn't be breached.

"I'm ready. Sammy will be here any moment."

Caileen turned from the kitchen window and smiled at her daughter, who had a backpack slung over one shoulder. "What time should I expect you tomorrow?"

Zia sighed. Loudly. "By noon."

"Great. You can have the car to go to the library. I'm going to work in the yard."

"You should hire someone to do the mowing. I know, we're saving for a new roof," Zia added glumly before Caileen could remind the girl of the harsh reality.

The doorbell rang.

"There's Sammy. See you tomorrow," Zia sang out and dashed for the door, the backpack swinging jauntily against her hip. "Uh, Mom, I think it's someone for you," she called a few seconds later.

Caileen went into the living room. Jeff Aquilon stood on the porch. "Hello," she said, flustered at seeing him.

He held up the books. "Krista finished these. I thought I would return them since I was in town."

Zia stepped back so he could enter. The room seemed much smaller with his presence. Noting the questions in her daughter's eyes, Caileen introduced the two.

"Mr. Aquilon is the guardian of two of my clients. Zia is my daughter," she explained to him.

"Call me Jeff," he said, shaking hands with the girl.

"Thank you," Zia said. Her smile was quick and dazzling. "There's a guy in my four o'clock history class at the university whose name is Aquilon."

"That would be my nephew, Jeremy," Jeff said, returning the smile. "He's finishing his senior year in high school, plus taking some college courses. He missed a year, so he's in a hurry to make it up."

"I see. Please, won't you have a seat?"

He glanced at Caileen. She indicated the easy chair and took her place at the end of the sofa.

Zia glanced out the door. "Here's Sammy. I have to run. Nice meeting you, Jeff."

With another one of her dazzling smiles, she was out the door and off on her grand adventure. Silence prevailed.

"Did Krista enjoy the stories?" Caileen asked.

"She did. I wondered if you could recommend others. Perhaps longer books. She went through those in two nights and could have done it in one if Wednesday hadn't been a school night."

"She has a high reading score, more than two

grades above the fifth-grade level. I should have remembered that."

"Is she gifted? Is that the word the academics use nowadays?"

"Yes, it is." She stared at him while she considered.

He wore dark slacks and a white shirt, the cuffs rolled up on his arms. The collar was open, revealing a white T-shirt. He looked fit and strong.

Forcing herself to look away, she told him, "I'll have to check her record, but I think she missed the standard tests for the gifted program last year."

"Can she take them now?"

Caileen shook her head. "It's only given once a year and only to fourth graders in elementary school."

He gave an exasperated snort. "Bureaucracy."

"You can have her tested, but you'll have to pay the costs. I can give you the names of the approved testing services so you can consult with them."

"Good. What do you think of the gifted program in the local school system?"

"Zia loved the field trips and advanced experiments they did, but some teachers just gave extra work to those in the program. The kids didn't think that was fair."

He grimaced. "Busywork. I'd hate that, too." He paused, then added on a thoughtful note, "Your daughter is quite beautiful." His gaze ran over her as if wondering where the beauty came from.

Caileen nodded. "She looks exactly like her father. Blond, curly hair. Blue eyes. Same shape face. The same tall, slender body. The energy. I always felt as if I were in a mysterious force field when I was with him. When things were good between us." She winced internally at the last phrase. She hadn't meant to say that at all.

"Things do change," he said casually.

"Yes. Sometimes I wish she could have stayed Krista's age."

"But kids grow up."

"And have minds of their own." She managed a smile.

Then, to her amazement, her eyes misted over as worry over her child assailed her. She blinked rapidly and got the errant tears under control as Jeff prepared to leave.

"Well, I suppose I'd better get home. Friday is Tony's night to cook dinner. It's always grilled hamburgers. Krista got after him about the fat content of the potato chips we used to have with them so we're having lime gelatin with pineapple chunks and grated carrots and grapes instead." He grinned somewhat wryly as he described the meal.

"That's nice," she said. Her voice wobbled.

"Are you okay?"

She nodded and burst into tears.

Chapter Three

Jeff reacted without thinking. He went to Caileen, sat beside her on the sofa and put an arm around her shoulders while she sobbed.

"I'm sorry," she whispered. "I'm just…overwhelmed right now."

"That's okay." He tried to think of a word that might apply to her problems, whatever they were. "Life seems unfair at times, but things have a way of working out." There, that sounded vaguely wise. And, he hoped, comforting.

"For better or for worse?" she questioned with more than an edge of bitterness.

The phrase from the traditional marriage vows

gave him a clue. "Have you recently broken off with someone?"

"No!"

She was so adamant he believed her at once. He couldn't think of anything else to say, so he shut up. When she rested partly against him and partly against the sofa back, he found he liked the weight of her body on his.

When she turned toward him, he could feel the pressure of her breast against his side, and the warmth of her leg against his. She laid her right arm across his lap while she slid the other between his back and the sofa.

His libido sprang to hot, hard and instant attention.

He tried to suck in his stomach so she wouldn't feel the pulsating ridge if she moved her arm just a fraction of an inch. Unfortunately he could only withdraw so far.

She sighed and leaned more into him. He knew the moment she became aware of his predicament.

Neither moved for a stunned moment, then she tilted her head against his shoulder, her eyes searching his as if bent on finding some great truth he was determined to hide.

He observed her, too. Her lips looked soft, full and inviting. They trembled with each breath. Her nose was pink on the tip, her eyes were red-rimmed and shimmering with unshed tears, and the moisture-laden lashes attractively outlined her eyes.

The color of her irises reminded him of the aqua green depths of the sea around the Caribbean islands he'd once explored while taking a special course in strategic sea tactics as a Ranger.

Her skin was smooth as he traced the tracks of the tears and dried them gently with his fingers. He ran one finger along her lips, which were soft to the touch and also vulnerable with the sorrow she evidently felt.

"What's bothering you?" he asked, his voice going deep and husky as the internal hunger increased.

"Zia."

"Kids and parents often have differences."

She nodded against his shoulder and sighed again. Her breath softly penetrated his shirt, bringing a flush to his skin and yearning throughout his body. He wanted to search that full, mobile mouth with his own, to find the sweetness he instinctively knew was there, waiting for him to taste.

Everything about her shouted *woman* to his starved senses. He shook his head slightly. Damn, but he must be on the verge of stark raving lunacy.

"Uh, Mrs. Peters…Caileen," he began, then stopped, not knowing where to go from there.

She tilted her head back again to gaze at him.

The movement cut right through the tether he'd managed to rope around his personal needs over the past months. He grabbed at the fraying ends of his control, but it was no use. Without thinking further, he bent his head and kissed her…and kissed her… and kissed her…

The touch of their lips, the pressure of their bodies against each other and the sheer pleasure in the embrace hit him on several levels at once. Excitement buzzed through his head, making his mind hazy, yet an odd sense of contentment settled like a blanket around his shoulders, shutting out the wintry chill of loneliness he hadn't known he had.

As he'd suspected—she was a tempting woman.

Caileen wasn't sure why she wasn't pulling back in shock and indignation at their mutual passion.

The feelings flooding through her combined bliss with anticipation, warmth with contentment and an excitement she hadn't experienced in a long time, nothing even close to shock and indignation.

"Ages," she murmured when his lips moved from her mouth to her ear, then down her jaw and to her throat. "It's been ages since I've felt this."

"Me, too," he admitted in a low growly tone that sent ripples along every nerve.

He stroked her back with gentle, soothing caresses, his touch at once tender and passionate and masterful. His eyes were dark and sexy and inviting. She wanted to dive right into those exciting depths and never come up.

"This is so odd," she told him. "It isn't like me at all." She sounded very uncertain. It occurred to her that maybe this moment was more closely linked to her true self than any other occurrence during the past few years.

Cupping her face in his hands, he peered into her eyes. "What are you like?" he asked.

"I'm very serious," she explained. "I consider every aspect of a situation. I—I don't go off the deep end like this. I'm not sure what we're doing…"

His chuckle was wry, as if he laughed at all human foibles, not just theirs. "Comforting each other, I think."

Put that way, it didn't sound so awful. Everyone could use a little compassion at times.

She inhaled sharply when his lips sought hers again. She felt his tongue sweep over her lips and opened her mouth so they could explore each other more thoroughly.

It was the nicest sensation, a soft, moist coming together that seemed just right for this moment in time…a time out of time, really.

When she raised her arm to stroke his chest through the smooth cotton of his shirt, he shifted them so that he leaned into the corner of the sofa and she rested across his lap. The change in position gave them more intimate access to each other. She liked that.

As they kissed, she explored the breadth of his shoulders and the strength of his biceps. When she caressed along his torso, his muscles tensed so that she felt the ripple effect of his toned abs.

"You're strong," she said when they came up

for breath, as if she'd just discovered this enchanting fact.

"It's my work," he murmured, placing tiny kisses all over her face. "And the sculptures. They're heavy."

"They're lovely." She kissed the heavily beating pulse in his throat. "I saw the statue of the maiden and the swan you made for the fountain in town. It was beautiful."

"Leda and the Swan, from Greek mythology. Did you know the swan was Zeus in disguise?"

"No."

"He changed form so he could seduce her."

Caileen drew back enough to gaze into his eyes. "Is that what you're doing to me?"

He shook his head, his gaze lambent, his smile oddly gentle. "I wouldn't try to trick a woman."

"Ah, an honest man."

"I hope so." His manner was rueful.

His voice dropped an octave, becoming deep and riveting with a rich sexual nuance. With something like shock, and yet she wasn't altogether surprised, she responded to him with a need so strong she wondered why she hadn't been aware of it in the past.

Because she hadn't met *this* man before now?

A shaky sigh escaped her as she gave herself to the passion and the moment, knowing this was insane, knowing tomorrow would bring regret—knowing and not caring.

* * *

Jeff forced himself from the honey of her mouth and gazed into her eyes. The irises were huge, indicative of the passion that raged between them. He knew his were the same.

He also knew she wasn't ready to follow the desire to its logical conclusion. He wasn't sure he was, either. To get involved with the person who had ultimate control over his life with the children was just plain stupid.

Reluctantly he let the blood cool between them until they could both think clearly once more. When she sat up, her manner reflected the confusion and dismay she felt at their indiscretion.

"I'm sorry," she said. "I'm so very sorry…"

He forced a smile. "I think that's where we were when this all started."

She nodded, her eyes wide and serious, as if she were in shock that she could have acted so wantonly. For some reason, that made him angry.

"Don't worry about it," he advised. "Even the coolest head can become overheated in the right circumstances."

"I'm not supposed to lose control," she said. "I'm supposed to take charge."

He rose, figuring he'd outstayed his welcome by a wide margin. "Look, this wasn't a very good start to what promises to be a long relationship. Call it an aberration of the moment. Anyway, let's put it behind us. Okay?"

She had to think this over for a long time, it seemed to him. "Yes. You're right," she said. "It was my fault. I've been worried.... But that isn't your problem." She shook her head slightly as if getting her mind on track once more. "Let me get those books."

He was almost angry again at her evident relief at getting back to business. She hurried over to a tall bookcase and removed three volumes. "Has Krista read any of the *Anne of Green Gables* books?"

"I don't know."

"Oh. Well, try these. I'll write down some titles next week. You can take her to the library and get her a card so she can check them out on her own. That would be a good thing—"

She stopped abruptly. Her eyes went to the sofa behind him. He wondered if she was thinking their kisses had been a good thing. As far as he was concerned, they had been.

Damn good. And damn stupid on his part.

It was obvious by the way she wouldn't quite meet his eyes that she felt the same. He heaved a weary sigh and bid her good night.

After taking the books and leaving the house, he drove home deep in thought. He couldn't alienate the tempting social worker. She was far too important in the life of his newly acquired family.

He realized he'd never considered that she might have worries of her own. He could sympathize with her concern over her daughter. It was far easier to tell others how to manage their affairs than figure out how to handle your own problems.

The evening had slipped into dusk by the time he arrived at the house. The lights inside beckoned him.

Going to the door, he saw the kids were in the living room, all with books in their hands, their faces identical expressions of concentration.

A surge of warmth hit his heart as he went inside.

He had to be careful, he realized. He couldn't do anything to jeopardize their right to live here, such as make a fool of himself over their counselor.

Caution was called for. He was good at strategy, he reminded himself sternly, and the best strategy was to keep his distance and maintain a grip on his libido.

Saturday morning, Caileen carried her coffee outside and sat under the vine-covered arbor. The sun was up, and the day was supposed to be warm. She basked in the peace and quiet. Her tenants—a young couple, both teachers—on the other side of the house usually slept late on the weekends, so she had the place to herself.

As soon as the neighbors were stirring, she would get the grass mowed and do some pruning of shrubs. She'd written up the reports she'd scheduled to do that morning, so she was caught up.

She'd also come to terms with her illogical behavior with Jeff. Worry. That's what it was. The passion had been a release of her pent-up fears.

To err is human; to forgive, divine.

Around midnight she'd taken the old adage to heart and decided to forgive the loss of control that led to her inappropriate actions of the previous evening. Besides, going over and over the event hadn't solved a thing.

Next, she'd determined to get some sleep. Amazingly, she'd fallen into bed and into a restful slumber. Although it was early, she felt as if she'd slept a solid eight hours and was ready for the new day.

An hour later, she pushed the reel-type mower through the grass and finished the backyard in record time. After mowing the tiny patch of lawn in front of the duplex, she worked the rest of the morning on pruning bushes and removing the mulch from flower beds so the sun could warm the ground and wake the plants from their winter's rest.

At noon, she showered and put on fresh slacks and a long-sleeved T-shirt, then ate a sandwich, again choosing to sit on the back porch.

Around the neighborhood, families worked on flower beds, washed cars or chatted over the low fences between yards. Caileen inhaled the wonderful aroma of fresh-cut grass and that of baking bread. Her neighbor two doors down loved to cook and favored everyone with the delicious results.

Caileen glanced at her watch. It was after one. Ignoring the faint maternal prod of concern, she decided to go to the grocery store while she still had the car.

After checking supplies and making a list, she drove to the supermarket and did the weekly shopping. She wondered how Tony's hamburgers and gelatin side dish had been received by Jeff and the other two.

In line at the checkout counter, she realized she was smiling as she thought of them. She touched her lips as if to be sure the smile was real. It was.

When it was her turn, she stacked the groceries on the moving belt and ran her credit card through the machine while Thelma, who'd worked there for the twelve years she'd lived in town, scanned the items. She was signing the credit slip when an ambulance rushed by, its siren warning others to clear a path. She and the clerk glanced up.

"I hope no one was injured in an accident." Thelma frowned and shook her head. "My grandson got arrested for drag racing last weekend. My son is thinking about grounding him for life."

"Teenagers can be reckless," Caileen agreed.

"Ah, well, they grow out of it."

Thelma finished bagging the groceries and loaded them onto the cart. Caileen left the store, her gaze going toward the street and the small hospital that served the community.

At the emergency portico, she saw the paramedics lift out a gurney and wheel it inside. The sunlight reflected from the plastic IV bag that dangled above the patient.

On the way home, she found herself dwelling on

the scene and realized it was worry over her daughter that troubled her. After all, a trip to the hospital could be a joyous occasion—for instance, the birth of a child.

She remembered how frightened she'd been on the way to the hospital to have her baby. She'd been not quite twenty-one years old and alone. Brendon had gotten a job at a construction site that summer and was working long hours.

At home, she stored the food, her mind still on the past. As inexperienced parents, she and her husband had been terrified of the tiny child now in their keeping, but they'd both fallen in love with her.

Caileen finished her task, then paused and considered those long-ago days and two months of fatigue before Zia had slept the night through. Brendon had been good about helping then. When had things gone wrong for them?

When she'd wanted a stable home and a steady source of income. When she'd decided it was time for them—both of them—to grow up.

Maybe she'd expected too much.

Before she could dwell on this, the telephone rang. She grabbed the wall phone at the end of the counter. "Hello?"

Expecting her daughter's voice, she was surprised when a masculine voice inquired, "Mrs. Peters?"

"Yes?"

"This is Sammy. Uh, Zia's been hurt."

"Hurt? How? Where is she?"

"At the hospital. You'd better come down. She asked for you before she, uh, passed out."

Caileen wanted to ask a hundred questions, but she refrained. "I'll be right there," she promised and hung up.

Grabbing her purse, she dug out the keys while she ran to the car. On the road, she wouldn't let herself go more than ten miles over the speed limit even though she wanted to floor the pedal. She parked at the curb near the emergency room and dashed inside.

"I'm Caileen Peters," she told the woman behind the admitting desk. "My daughter, Zia, was brought in a short time ago?" Her voice trailed upward into a question.

"Mmm, Peters, yes. The surgeon is with her. I have some forms for you to sign."

"What happened?" Caileen demanded, ignoring the forms as panic rose inside her. "Why is she in surgery?"

"A car accident," the woman said sympathetically. "Your daughter is doing fine. Her blood pressure stabilized shortly after the ambulance crew put the IV in. The floor nurse will be with you in a minute. She'll give you a full report."

Caileen digested the information while a hundred questions whirled through her mind.

The woman held out a pen. "Fill out the form and sign at the bottom. Do you have insurance?"

"Yes, through the county. I'm with Family Services."

Her hand trembling slightly, Caileen signed the papers. When she was finished, a nurse told her Zia was in surgery to repair a torn blood vessel. "But what happened?" she asked. "How did she get injured?"

"A piece of metal hit her in the neck, causing a jagged edge to nick an artery," the nurse said gently. "Your daughter was lucky that no other damage was done. Here's the waiting room. The surgeon will see you when he's finished. Your daughter's friend is here, too."

Caileen went into the quiet, tastefully furnished room. The aroma of fresh coffee filled the air. "Sammy," she said, spotting the handsome young man sitting in a kitchen chair at a table. "What happened?"

He avoided her eyes. "There was an accident."

"In your pickup?"

He hesitated, then shook his head. "Two of the guys were, uh, sort of racing. They sideswiped each other and a piece of chrome flew off and hit Zia on the side of her neck."

"Drag racing?" Caileen asked, recalling the grocery clerk's remarks.

Sammy nodded. "A lot of people use the old back road, the one near the campground, to check out their engines. We were standing beside the road, watching."

Caileen suppressed the anger his words caused. Now wasn't the time to accuse him of putting her child in danger. Zia had gone of her own accord. "What happened after the injury?"

"She was bleeding a lot," he said, gesturing helplessly. "I held a handkerchief against the wound while someone called the ambulance on a cell phone."

Caileen stared at his hands as he clasped them and leaned forward, his forearms on his thighs. He had large hands, a man's hands, but his expression was that of a boy who'd been caught in some mischief. He was twenty-one, an adult by law. She sighed and poured a cup of coffee, then took a seat opposite him.

Another person came into the room. She glanced up and her eyes met those of Jeff Aquilon. She stared at him.

He nodded, walked over to the counter and got a cup of coffee, then stopped by the table. "May I join you?" he asked.

"Yes. What are you doing here?" She realized how rude that sounded. "Is everything all right?"

"With my family, yes. The hospital called and asked if Jeremy and I could give blood. We're both O negative."

"Universal donors," Sammy said.

"Zia is A negative," Caileen said, trying to put all these facts together into a whole.

"I understand she was injured in a car accident," Jeff said. His gaze settled on Sammy. "You should know better than to bring women along when you're doing something stupid."

Caileen was surprised when Sammy's ears and face reddened. "We always have meets on the weekends. No one ever got injured before," he said defensively.

"Yeah," Jeff said in an unforgiving tone. "There's always a first time, and then you learn."

"You gave blood for Zia?" Caileen asked, interrupting the other two.

The dark eyes flicked to her. "Yes."

"Your nephew is giving blood, too?"

"Yes."

A rush of gratitude flowed through her. "Thank you," she said. "That was kind of you. And your nephew."

He shrugged. "We're on a special call list with the hospital. Blood supplies are low due to lack of donors." Again his hard gaze settled on the younger man. "You should persuade your friends to come down and give blood. That way, you can make up in part for the harm you've caused."

Sammy swallowed, his throat working as though he'd bitten off a large bite and was having trouble getting it down. "I will," he said hoarsely.

Caileen felt sorry for him. He looked as if he might burst into tears at any moment.

"And you can apologize to her mother."

Caileen didn't know what to say as Sammy apologized for putting her daughter in danger. "Thank you," she finally murmured when Sammy stopped his faltering apology. "However, Zia is an adult. I suppose she chose to be there."

"Maybe, maybe not," Jeff spoke before Sammy

could. "Even an independent woman trusts her boyfriend to take care of her. Right?" He narrowed his eyes and stared at Sammy.

"Yes, sir."

Caileen almost expected Sammy to stand at attention and salute. The tense little scene was interrupted by the arrival of Jeff's nephew. He walked into the room with a bandage around his elbow.

"Sit here," his uncle advised. "You want some juice? The nurse said there was plenty in the fridge."

Jeremy took the chair. "Please." He looked Sammy over. "You the guy who took her to the illegal drag race?"

That he didn't think much of the other young man was clear. Sammy nodded, looking miserable. Caileen kept her mouth shut.

"Are you Zia's mother?" he asked after thanking his uncle for a box of orange juice. He stuck a straw in it and took a long drink.

"Yes, I am," Caileen answered. She studied Jeff and Jeremy, noting how alike they were with their dark, dark eyes, thick, brown-black hair and serious air. "You have a class with her at college, I understand."

Jeremy smiled. It did wonders for his face, just the way Jeff's smiles lit up his countenance, she noticed.

"Yeah. She's one smart kid."

Caileen smiled and agreed. It was amusing to hear this young man call her daughter a kid. From her info on the family, she knew Jeremy was three months younger than Zia.

However, he seemed older, Caileen acknowledged. He'd taken on the responsibility of protecting his younger cousins—step-cousins actually—last year and had cared for them with no outside help for months.

She glanced at Jeff, who silently observed the exchange. He was a person who didn't duck his responsibility to his family, either. Like uncle, like nephew?

For a second, she wished her child would find someone like Jeremy to date. And for a second longer, she wished she'd found someone like Jeff when she was nineteen and idealistic…

The doctor came in just then. "Mrs. Peters?"

She stood. "Yes?"

A large warm hand found hers. She glanced at Jeff, who'd also risen and was standing beside her. She stared at the surgeon in dread.

"Zia is fine. She's weak from the loss of blood, but she's young and healthy. She'll be ready to go home in the morning. I don't expect any complications."

Caileen nodded. She realized she was squeezing the life out of Jeff's hand and let go, embarrassed at clinging to him as if she were one of those neurotic TV mothers.

The doctor glanced at Sammy. "There's a policeman in the lobby wanting a statement from you."

Going pale, Sammy rose and hurried down the corridor to the main lobby.

"Thanks to both of you for coming in," the doctor continued, his eyes on Jeff and Jeremy.

"It was no trouble," Jeff assured him.

"Yeah, but next time tell the nurse not to use that rusty needle," Jeremy quipped, giving his bandaged arm a pained glance.

The two men chuckled, a pleasant sound that eased the tension gripping her, she found.

"Well, we have work to do," Jeff said. He glanced at her. "Since Zia will be here overnight, why don't you come out and have dinner with us, say, around six-thirty?"

"Thanks, but I think I should stay here in case Zia needs anything."

His dark gaze studied her for another second, then he nodded and left the room with his nephew.

"It was a good thing we had those two to call on," the doctor told her. "The transfusions will give Zia the boost she needs. Her blood pressure was pretty low. By tomorrow, she'll be nearly as good as new."

From the window, she watched Jeff and Jeremy cross the hospital parking lot to a pickup. "They saved her life."

The surgeon smiled. "They certainly helped."

She turned to him. "I can't thank you enough for your help. May I see her now?"

"She's in recovery. The nurse will come for you as soon as your daughter is taken to a room."

Caileen thanked him again and returned to her

chair to wait. A couple of minutes after he left, another man entered the silent waiting room.

"I thought you might like company while you wait," Jeff told her.

Her eyes filled with tears at this unexpected kindness.

"Hey, none of that. You know where it leads." He gave her a rakish grin.

Her chin wobbled, but she laughed. She did indeed recall where her tears had gotten them the previous evening.

During those moments in his arms, she'd been swept up in an illusion, one that whispered it might be possible for her to be happy and carefree and in love once more.

The summons for her to come to the hospital to see about her daughter had been a reminder of the harsh facts of life. Neither love nor passion made the world go 'round.

If only she could convince Zia to get her head out of the clouds and focus on her future, then things would be easier for her.

But maybe that kind of thinking only came from experience. Painful experience.

Summoning patience, she settled down to wait, aware of the man who waited with her and the quiet strength that seemed to flow from him to her. She ignored the feeling. She, too, had to keep her sights fixed on terra firma.

Chapter Four

Sunday evening, Caileen set the table with her favorite pottery dishes and stepped back to view the effect. The festive colors—red, hot pink, green, gold and deep blue in floral swirls—perked up her spirits and calmed her nerves.

She was a little tense about having the Aquilon family over for dinner, but Zia wanted to thank Jeff and Jeremy for their help and Caileen had agreed a meal would be appropriate. She glanced toward the sofa, her heart squeezing into its usual ball of worry when she contemplated her offspring.

Zia, her feet propped on the ottoman and the laptop computer on a pillow across her lap, was busily working on the term paper that was due the next day. Stacked around her were the books and notes that Caileen had fetched from her daughter's room or the car or the library.

The girl looked quite lovely in a fleecy blue outfit that matched her eyes. Her blond hair lay in shining waves rather than curly ringlets, thanks to blow-drying. Her face was still pale from the loss of blood, but she'd put on mascara and a soft pink lipstick, so she didn't look washed out. The small bandage on the side of her neck gave no clue to the seriousness of the accident.

"Thirty minutes," Caileen said.

"Yes, Mother, I'm watching the time," Zia retorted, but with indulgent humor rather than irritation.

Caileen's smile conceded her tendency to worry. She wanted the dinner to be pleasant. After turning the chicken pieces that were marinating in a mixture of wine vinegar and spices, she checked the salads and vegetables she'd prepared, then peered into the oven where the bread pudding, which would be served with hot custard sauce, was browning to perfection.

The ringing of the doorbell stopped her chaotic musing. Warmth hit her cheeks at the same instant an electric tingle surged through her breasts. Her nipples hardened, their outline clearly visible against the lacy pattern of her emerald-green sweater. She instinctively crossed her arms over the telltale sign of agitation.

"Mother," Zia called out, obviously wondering why she wasn't hurrying to the door.

Caileen ran her palms down the black slacks she

wore, put on her best hostess smile and went to the living room to admit the Aquilon family into her home. "Hello. Please come in." She opened the door wide and stepped aside so they could enter.

Jeff, then Jeremy, stepped inside. They were the same height, the nephew a slighter version of the more muscular man. Tony and his sister came next. The boy, as slender as a willow sapling, was already within a couple of inches in matching the other two men in height.

Krista projected the leggy leanness inherent in the males of her blended family. Like Zia and herself, the girl would be taller than the average woman.

All four looked so much alike that she was sure many people mistook them for a father and his three children.

"I hope we aren't too early," Jeff said.

She closed the door and glanced at the clock. "No. You're exactly on time. I was just checking the menu to make sure I hadn't forgotten anything."

"Once she left a whole bowl of green beans in the fridge when my grandparents were here for Thanksgiving," Zia piped up. "We ate them for days after they left."

Jeff turned his gaze on the girl. His smile was like a gift, Caileen thought. There was a seriousness in it that spoke of responsibility…and caring.

"How are you feeling today?" he asked.

"Tired and achy," Zia admitted. "I didn't realize

that losing blood could make you feel as if you had the flu."

"It can," he affirmed as one who'd also been through a life-and-death ordeal. "Your body also absorbed the trauma of several pieces of flying metal. That's probably what made you sore."

Caileen gestured toward the chairs. "Please, take a seat. I have some warm spiced tea to take the chill off the evening. Our department manager served it at Christmas and everyone thought it was delicious. She gave me the recipe."

She realized she was talking too much and fled to the kitchen. From the living room, she heard Jeff introduce Tony and Krista to Zia, a task she should have performed.

Jeremy asked about the paper Zia was working on for the history class and said he'd finished his yesterday.

Caileen ran cold water over her wrists and hands as sweat beaded on her face and between her breasts, desperate to quell the odd case of nerves and the flash of desire that had reverberated through her upon seeing Jeff.

"Can I help?" a masculine voice broke into her feverish thoughts.

She jerked around. Jeff stood in the archway between the kitchen and dining room, his hands in his pockets, his manner relaxed. Obviously *he* wasn't shaken at the sight of *her*. She turned off the faucet and dried her hands.

"Uh, yes. If you'll take those cups, I'll carry these. Would you like some brandy in your tea? Sometimes I put a drop in. On a cold night. Especially during a storm."

She pressed her lips firmly together.

"That sounds good, but I'll refrain tonight. With the kids here, I suppose we should set an example."

"Yes. Of course." She felt as if she'd made a terrible social blunder in suggesting the brandy.

"Now if this *were* a winter night with a cold wind blowing outside and a fire going inside," he said, his tone teasing, but his eyes dark and fathomless as if other thoughts filled his mind, "and if we were alone…"

He let the words trail into silence, then picked up three mugs with parrots painted on them in a riot of colors and carried them into the living room. Flustered, Caileen followed, handing a mug to Jeremy and one to Zia. She rushed to the kitchen for the remaining one.

Turning, she nearly ran into Jeff. The hot tea sloshed from side to side in the mug but didn't spill.

"Sorry. I didn't mean to startle you." He took the mug from her trembling hand and placed it on the counter. "Is it time to put the chicken on? I'm a whiz on the grill, if you would like my expert advice and/or aid."

His rumble of laughter was low and sinful, as if they shared some wonderful secret. She laughed, too.

"I would love it. I bought a new grill on special last fall and frankly I've never used it."

"Gas or charcoal?" he asked.

She led the way to the patio. "Gas. I thought we would use it more since charcoal takes so long to heat up. Which do you use?"

"Gas, and for the same reason. I never remembered to start the briquettes until I was ready to cook."

They went outside after she flicked on the light. The vine-covered arbor protected them from the evening wind, but the air was still chilly. She wrapped her arms across her torso while he inspected the grill.

In a few seconds, he had the fire going. "It needs to heat up five or ten minutes before we put the food on," he told her.

They reached for the doorknob at the same moment. His hand, big and capable and strong, closed over hers. His chest touched her shoulder as he leaned forward. Their lips, she realized with a start, were inches apart.

When she looked into his eyes, she felt as if she were being swept into a whirlwind. The hot intensity of his gaze flashed a lightning trail straight down to some very private, very reserved part of her. It burned away the barriers erected from past experience and made her gasp.

"Me, too," he said. His frown was perplexed, as if he couldn't figure out the attraction.

"What?" she asked, unwilling to admit to the odd feelings swirling inside.

"You know. Don't pretend," he murmured.

She sighed loudly. "I can't figure it out."

His chuckle was sardonic. "Oh, I think I understand this part of it." He touched her cheek, ran his fingers along her jaw and under her chin. With the gentlest of pressure, he raised her face to his.

Still gazing into her eyes, he kissed her—not too hard, or she would have drawn back; not too soft, or she would have thought he was mocking her. On a scale of one to ten as kisses go, it was a perfect ten.

"It's the rest of it that's worrisome," he said, moving back a few inches.

"I'm the counselor on your case," she reminded him, an accusation in her tone, as if he were solely responsible for the passion between them.

The frown deepened. "Yeah, I know. What I didn't realize was that you would be this tempting or that I would be so susceptible." With a grim smile, he moved the hand that still covered hers.

Mustering what dignity she could, she went inside, and he followed a respectable two feet behind. The stereo played soft music. Zia's laughter mingled with that of their guests. The aroma of food was reassuring, as if all were normal in this safe, indoor world.

Which was true. She was the one off-kilter.

Jeff lifted the platter of chicken. "Anything else to go on the grill?"

"Uh, not now. I'll bring out the bread in a minute."

He nodded and returned to the grill. She refilled the young people's mugs before spreading garlic butter on French bread slices. When she took the bread outside, Jeff was studying the night sky.

"Would you put these on the warming rack?" she asked, keeping a polite distance from him.

"Sure."

The flash of his smile acknowledged their return to hostess and guest status.

Good. She liked things straightforward and…and clear-cut, so everyone knew his or her place in the grand scheme of things. Although of late she seemed to have lost her way, she admitted upon reentering the house.

Ten minutes passed. The back door opened. Jeff entered, carrying two platters. He elbowed the door shut. "Dinner, madam," he intoned in a deep voice that sent vibrations down her spine and into that private place.

She realized she'd been standing in the middle of the kitchen, apparently in a trance, since finishing her chores. "Thank you," she muttered. "I think everything is ready."

He stood aside while she placed the food on a sideboard, then called the others to the table. "Take that end," she told Jeff.

It wasn't until everyone was seated—Jeremy gallantly helped Zia to her chair—that Caileen realized how the table arrangement would look to an outsider.

With her in the hostess seat and Jeff on the opposite end, with Zia and Jeremy on one side and Tony and Krista on the other, it appeared to be the ideal family scene.

The tears that seemed forever at the back of her throat these days stung her nose and eyes. "I think Zia wanted to say something," she announced.

Zia beamed at Jeremy, then at Jeff, her gaze lingering on the older man as she thanked them for coming to the hospital and donating blood for her.

"Now that your blood is flowing in me, I think that means I'm yours for life," she ended, laughing in an intriguing manner and giving Jeff a teasing glance from under her long lashes.

Uneasiness shot through Caileen.

"It was our civic and moral duty," Jeff said, easily deflecting the hero worship. "We're always on call in case of accidents."

Caileen relaxed. One thing she knew about Jeff Aquilon—he was an honorable man.

"You can thank me by writing my next term paper," Jeremy said to break the tiny silence.

"Like that's going to happen," Zia told him.

Jeremy shrugged good-naturedly. "A guy can hope."

Caileen passed the platters of food and the conversation became general as Zia asked the two youngsters about their teachers. Since she'd attended the same school system, she knew all the ins and outs and earnestly advised them on getting the best teachers and on which classes to take when both said they intended to go to college.

"Like Jeremy," Krista added in her shy way.

Caileen looked from the girl to her uncle. Jeff's eyes met hers. He nodded slightly, admitting he knew the young girl had a crush on her stepcousin. His smile indicated he had no problems with that.

Neither did she, she realized. Jeremy was much older than his years and very protective of the younger two. From what she'd seen so far, he and his uncle would provide good role models for the girl.

She gazed at Jeff, again wishing her young husband had had some of those steady qualities. A fleeting sadness for what could never be flicked through her, leaving her wondering why she was having such thoughts of late.

Catching Zia's eyes on her, Caileen smiled at her lovely, charming daughter, pleased that the evening was going as well as she'd hoped it would. Zia looked away.

Caileen sensed her daughter's disapproval and was taken aback. Now what had she done?

After the dessert, which was a big hit with everyone, Caileen noticed Jeff's gaze on Zia. She, too, studied her daughter, who'd sparkled with charm all evening.

The nineteen-year-old was definitely pale. Her smile was not so bright and her responses were not as quick as they'd been earlier. Caileen refrained from putting a hand to her daughter's forehead to check for fever.

As soon as everyone was finished, Jeff stood. "We need to get on the road. Tomorrow is a school day, and it's past our bedtime."

His smile was dazzling when he turned it on Caileen. Her heart bobbed around unnecessarily. She sternly ordered it to quiet down.

"That was the best bread pudding I've ever eaten," he continued. "Everything was delicious."

"I'm so glad you could join us," Caileen said, her glance taking in all the Aquilons. She led the way to the door. "Oh, I have some more books for Krista, also for Tony."

She handed the books to the children, hesitated, then shook hands with Jeff and bid them good night. They called farewells to Zia, who still sat at the table.

After locking the door behind their guests, Caileen went to the patient and laid a hand on her forehead. "You feel a little warm."

Zia moved her head away, then surprised Caileen by saying, "Can you help me to my room? I feel a little dizzy."

"You stayed up too long. Perhaps we shouldn't have had guests so soon."

"Please. Don't get in the mother mode."

"I am your mother," Caileen said, offering her arm.

Zia held on while they walked down the hall and into her room. Caileen removed the teddy bear that held pride of place in the middle of the pillows, a gift from Brendon that he'd won at a fair when their daughter was ten, and turned down the bed. She acted busy until Zia had changed to pajamas and was safely tucked under the covers.

Whether her stubborn daughter liked it or not, she leaned down and kissed her cheek, feeling such a storm of maternal love and worry that the ridiculous tears threatened her poise once more.

"'Night, bedbug," she whispered, using an old childhood nickname.

"'Night, Mom." Zia closed her eyes wearily.

After cleaning up the kitchen, Caileen turned out the lights and headed for her own room. Once in bed, she stared into the dark and listened to the soft sounds of night.

The wind in the cottonwoods made a rustling murmur like rain on dried grass. It was a lonely sound....

She realized the loneliness came from within herself. For the first time since Brendon had walked out, leaving her with the bills to pay and their child to raise, she worried whether she was going to make it.

In fact, she didn't know what was eating at her. Closing her eyes, she willed the doubts to go away. Of course she was going to make it. Her life was fine.

If she could just keep Zia focused on finishing college rather than running off with the love of her life.

If the roof would hold out until she had saved enough money to get it replaced before next winter.

If she didn't have a total nervous breakdown before she could accomplish these goals.

If. If. If.

None of the projects seemed too certain at this point.

Jeff turned off the welding torch and studied the wrought-iron gate he was making for the client of a local home decorator/designer. The piece was mostly straight lines, other than three stylized pine trees in the center.

He liked the simplicity of the design. If only his life would follow a similar pattern, he would be perfectly happy.

A sigh worked its way up from deep inside him. Nothing was ever simple. Take last night. He hadn't been able to sleep once the kids were tucked into bed and all was silent in the house.

Why? Because the bed had suddenly seemed too big and too empty.

An image filled his mental vision. Worried green eyes, enhanced by a lacy sweater of the same color. Nervous hands that had trembled ever so slightly during the evening. A sweet womanly shape that he wanted to explore as he would a perfectly carved statue made from the finest marble.

In other words, Caileen Peters.

Naturally she was the one person in the world he shouldn't—couldn't—become involved with. She had the last word on Tony and Krista. He wouldn't do anything to jeopardize their safety, which in his opinion meant living with him so that he knew they were okay.

Tell that to his libido.

He'd lain awake, aware of needs he'd ignored the past year while the kids settled in, and thought of the pretty counselor for hours. He snorted in disgust at his lack of control.

Okay, so he was attracted.

Sooner or later, the hunger would fade—if he ignored it. Like a bad case of the flu, he'd recover and all would be well. Yeah.

Instead of getting on with his work, he wondered if the fact that he was missing a foot would bother her. The first woman he'd dated when he'd returned home from the army had turned from him in pity and revulsion.

That had hurt, and he'd become more cautious in his dealings with women. So, he would back off, be extra wary of the attraction and all would be well. Now if his body would only cooperate.

The drone of a car engine distracted him. The home designer had arrived to check on the progress of the gate. He went to the shop door to greet her.

Karen Bennett was a striking redhead with a perfect complexion and a sexy, stylish manner of dressing, but she was too thin in his estimation. He thought of Caileen's feminine curves.

"Damn," he muttered, breaking the erotic thought.

"Hi. Did you say something?" Karen called out.

He smiled and shook his head. "You're just in time. The gate is ready for the powdercoat."

"That's what I came to check on. We'll be ready to put it up come Thursday."

He gestured for her to enter the shop, then led the way to the welding area. "Is this what you wanted?"

"It's perfect. My clients will be thrilled. They're really into the three pines theme. That's what they're going to call their estate—Three Pines Farm."

"Farm? What are they going to grow on ten acres?"

She gave him a droll grin. "They're city dudes. Anything over an acre is a farm or ranch to them."

As she moved around the sculptured piece, Jeff caught the scent of her floral perfume. Caileen, he'd noted last night, liked a spicy blend. He realized that was his preference, too.

"Will you get the color on in time?"

"Sure. No problem."

She surprised him with a light pat on his cheek. "Thank you so much for your efforts on this. It was your idea of using the tree detail in the gate and the front fence on each side of the entry that sold them on my overall plan. I owe you."

He shook his head. "We local business people have to help each other all we can."

"Before the big chain stores come in and take over," she added with a grimace.

"That's business, too," he reminded her.

"Yeah, nothing personal, but excuse me while I put you out of business."

"I wouldn't think that would be a problem for a designer such as yourself. Yours is a special talent."

She flashed him a smile of thanks for the compliment. "Do you have time for a break? I could use a cup of coffee."

"Sure. This way."

He led the way to the house, giving credit to the kids when she exclaimed over the landscaping. Inside, he put on a fresh pot of coffee and offered her an apple tart. He wasn't surprised when she declined the treat.

"I don't think you have to worry about gaining weight," he said as he helped himself to a hefty piece.

"All women worry about their weight," she informed him. Her smile belied her words.

They sat at the counter when the coffee was ready and chatted about the area.

"There're new developments going up everywhere, it seems," she told him. "That's good for me, but I wonder where the people are coming from. And where they're getting their money. Everyone moving in appears to be wealthy."

Jeff swallowed a bite of the tart. "Technology attracts a high-end clientele. Boise has done well in enticing companies to the city. The executives all want five or ten acres in the country with a modern home and a horse or two in the pasture."

She laughed and agreed. "And what do you want?"

Although her tone was a sexy invitation to share confidences, he wasn't inclined to bare his soul. He shrugged. "A quiet place to work. A snug roof over my head. Enough to eat." He indicated the now empty dessert plate. "My needs are simple."

"As are mine."

He doubted that. She looked expensive in terms of money, time and effort on a man's part, but maybe he was taking things too seriously. At any rate, he knew he wasn't interested in even a brief fling with her.

He nodded, then made a point of checking the clock. "I've got to get back to work if you want that gate finished this week. I'll bring it to the site Thursday morning."

"That would be great. Thanks for the coffee."

He escorted her to her car, opening and closing the door, then standing aside as she waved. As she turned toward the road, relief washed over him when she was gone.

Right now wasn't a good time to get involved with a woman. He had too many irons in the fire. Literally.

He smiled as he turned on the welding arc and donned his helmet. He flipped the face protector into place and added the finishing touches to the metal gate.

Too bad it wasn't as easy to put protection around the heart. He'd always been a sucker for a hard-luck story.

Being with Caileen and her beautiful daughter last night, he'd seen the worry in the mother's eyes each time she'd glanced at the girl. He could understand that. Zia was at the stage where she was ready to try her wings. She was also curious about her power of attraction and had flirted with him during dinner.

It had been rather amusing, but he'd steered clear of her machinations. Her attentions should have been focused on Jeremy, but for some reason they seemed to rub each other the wrong way.

He considered his reaction to Caileen and hers to him. It was too bad that they rubbed each other in exactly the right way. If circumstances had been different…

Thinking of his empty bed and the restlessness of the night caused hunger to eat a hole in his resolution to keep his distance. Maybe it was time for a woman in his life. The kids could probably use a feminine role model.

Karen was thirty-five, divorced and interested. She'd seen his prosthetic foot once when she stopped by and found him in cutoffs while gardening. She apparently wasn't put off by that or the fact that he had three kids to raise.

He tried to picture the designer in a nurturing role, but the image wouldn't materialize. Instead he kept seeing Caileen bringing the books for Krista, worrying about her very beautiful, very precocious child, serving them a wonderful dinner and being as gracious as a hostess as she was considerate as a counselor.

What was he thinking? The Family Services representative was out of the picture. Definitely.

"Live with it," he advised his libido.

Chapter Five

Caileen made sure all the doors were locked before she left for the Friday morning meeting at the office. Zia was sleeping late, something she'd been doing all week, although she was usually a morning person.

Like mother, like daughter.

Taking a deep breath of the crisp April air, Caileen experienced the wonderful buoyancy of spring and wished she could take the day off to maybe hike along the river or simply sit in the backyard and read for hours and hours.

Fat chance.

She backed out of the drive and headed for work. At least she had no homes to visit today and only one brief court appearance that morning. In the afternoon she'd catch up on the onerous, never-ending paperwork.

In fact, she could stay late at the office since Sammy was bringing a pizza over for Zia and they planned to watch some videos. She'd call at noon and tell Zia or leave a message in case she went to her afternoon classes as she had yesterday.

Pulling into a parking space at the county office building, Caileen called a greeting to the department manager, then went to help the other woman bring in a load of manuals.

"The new marriage course," Susan Wynn said. "It teaches couples how to have a successful marriage in ten easy lessons. If only," she added.

Caileen smiled at the cynical note. "I'm glad Nan is the lucky one who gets to teach it."

"Uh, more about that in the meeting," Susan said with a pitying glance as Caileen unlocked and held open the door to the small suite of rooms Family Services occupied.

"Susan," Caileen said in a warning tone.

"Nan had her baby last night."

"She isn't due for two months."

"Tell that to the stork."

A horrifying thought came to Caileen. "You're not assigning me to the couples' class, are you?"

"You're the only one I trust to take over. The other counselors don't have the experience you do."

"Uh, don't you think it's a bit ironic to have a divorcée teach a class on making marriage work?

Besides, I was only married for five years and haven't had a serious relationship since."

"So? Maybe you'll get some ideas."

Leaving Susan to chortle alone, Caileen went to her own cubbyhole, locked her purse in a drawer, checked her notes on the custody case coming up at eleven and tried not to think about having to stay late at work one night a week for the next ten weeks. At nine, she attended the weekly conference of the counselors.

The meeting was relatively brief, and Caileen graciously accepted the new assignment while noting the relief in the other three counselors' eyes. Nan, the new mother—thank goodness it wasn't her, Caileen thought—would be on leave for six months; her cases were distributed among the three younger workers.

Later, heading for juvenile court, Caileen thought maybe one night a week of classes was better than having fifteen additional cases to handle. Inside the courtroom, she studied her notes again. She didn't want another reprimand from the juvenile judge.

After hearing the details of the case, the judge asked her for recommendations. Caileen was ready.

"The children could be left with the parents," she began, earning a frown from the grandparents and their attorney, "provided the couple attend a ten-week class on marriage management which will meet once a week at Family Services, and also provided they are willing to work with us on their parenting skills through counseling."

After asking several questions, the judge made sure the parents would work with the counselors, then assigned the children to them and scheduled a return appearance in three months to assess the family's progress.

Caileen added the court date plus weekly visits to the couple's home to her day planner. The visits would mean another late night each week for three months since she had no spare time until after her regular office hours. Ah, well, what was another two hours in the eternal spin of the universe? Not even a snap of the fingers.

Once outside, she waited in the shade of an oak tree until her best friend, Heather, who was a paralegal for the judge, finished her tasks and came out.

"Molly's?" Heather asked.

Caileen nodded. The restaurant was off the main drag and frequented by the locals. The food was good and inexpensive.

After they were seated, Heather asked, "Long day?"

"More work."

"Ah, that accounts for the heavy sigh. It sounds as if the world has grown heavier."

"Right. I think it's your turn to carry it."

Heather, also a single mother but with twin boys, age thirteen, had her share of troubles. They joked about whose turn it was to carry the load.

"With two boys entering puberty, I've got plenty. Cam's voice cracked the other day. It shocked all of us. Carl got a pimple. I found him going through all my toiletries trying to find something to get rid of it."

The two friends smiled in sympathy at each other.

Heather bent close. "Who's the good-looking guy staring at you?"

Startled by the change in subject, Caileen surveyed the crowded room. Her eyes met those of Jeff Aquilon. He was sitting with the most gorgeous redhead Caileen had ever seen. She was model slender and dressed in an elegant pantsuit in a shimmering copper color.

Jeff wore jeans and a tan suede jacket over a blue shirt, which was open at the throat. He looked elegant and rugged at the same time, with a city polish that she hadn't noticed before. His cosmopolitan air made her feel funny, as if she'd missed an important part of him.

He gave her a pleasant nod in greeting. Caileen returned his smile and widened it to include the redhead, who was observing them with open interest.

"I recognize the woman—she has an interior design shop here in town—but who's the man?" Heather asked.

"He's the foster father of two of my charges."

"So he and the redhead are married." Heather looked distinctly disappointed.

Caileen shook her head. "He's probably doing some work for her." She explained his business to her friend.

"Handsome as sin *and* talented," Heather murmured. "I may have palpitations."

Her friend's melodrama helped soothe Caileen's nerves as Jeff bid the woman goodbye, paid the check, then came over to their table, iced-tea glass in hand.

"Hello," he said. "May I join you?"

"Of course." Caileen introduced him to Heather. After the women had given their order to the waitress, she gazed at him, sensing he had a question.

"I want to ask your advice," he said. "It's about Krista."

"Yes?"

"Last night, after we finished reading, she mentioned she was having trouble with a classmate. At recess, all the kids have to participate in an activity, such as kickball or freeze tag. This girl waits until Krista joins a game, then comes over and tells her to leave."

"If there's bullying on the playground, we advise students to tell the teacher right away so she can put a stop to it," Caileen told him.

"Krista doesn't want to do that."

"It's tough to rat on someone. Has there been any physical abuse, shoving or anything like that?"

"Krista says no, just threats to make her eat a bug if she doesn't do as the girl tells her."

Heather rolled her eyes. "This sounds like my boys. I have thirteen-year-old twins," she explained to Jeff.

"Is the girl backed up by friends?" Caileen asked.

"Yeah. There are always two others with her."

"Cliques can be mean and more dangerous than one person acting alone. I can suggest a couple of strategies for Krista, but if they don't work, the teacher, and perhaps the principal, should be informed."

He nodded. "What should she do?"

"First she can try to include the girls in the game by inviting them to join the group before they can act against her. If that doesn't work, she can invite a friend to go do something else with her. She has to sound cheerful and confident while doing this as if it doesn't bother her at all. You can practice it with her."

"Then what?" he asked.

"That usually will draw others to her and away from the bullies. Children know those types can turn on anyone at any moment, so they avoid them as much as possible."

"That sounds like a lot to put on a kid," he said.

"It is," she admitted.

"Bullies have to be faced," Heather told him, then turned to Caileen. "What if Krista refused to leave? Or asked the others if they want her to go?"

"Put it to a vote?" Caileen thought it over. "That puts the other students on the spot. They might not want to get involved or draw the bullies' wrath down on themselves."

"Tony offered to beat them up, but I don't think that's the wisest solution. Anything else?" he asked.

"Krista could decline to leave, but defuse the situation by telling the three they can join in if they want. That shifts the onus to them to be cooperative. If they refuse, she should go on with the game as if there were no interruption," Caileen suggested.

"Okay," Jeff said. "That gives me some options to pass on to her. Thanks for the help."

After he left, Heather sighed. "I wish I'd met him first," she complained.

"If you're interested, be my guest."

Her friend shook her head. "Not a chance. I saw the way he looked at you. In spite of the redhead, he couldn't take his eyes off you while they ate."

"Oh, really," Caileen scoffed.

"I'm serious." Heather quickly crossed her heart. "Use it or lose it, is what I always say. Don't you think he's worth a twirl?"

Caileen felt the heat hit her face like a slap with a hot, wet towel.

"Umm, I see you agree," Heather said, clamping a napkin over her mouth to stifle her laughter. "You're an attractive single woman. Why shouldn't you go for him?"

"Don't we have enough problems in our lives without adding a relationship that has nowhere to go?"

Heather tilted her head and narrowed her eyes while perusing Caileen. "Why does it have no place to go?"

Caileen shrugged. "I don't have time."

"You've already written off what could be the greatest thing in your sad, boring life, counselor."

"That's part of the problem. I'm the case worker for two children under his care."

"Jeez, handsome, talented and caring. What more could a person ask for?"

"Having a man is not the be-all, end-all of a woman's life," Caileen informed her friend.

Heather's expression mocked this lofty statement, then she became serious. "No, it isn't. We've both made it for years without anyone, but it's nice to think there may be a perfect man lurking about, waiting to be discovered."

"There isn't."

Her friend knew when to change the subject. "So how's Zia doing since the accident?"

They discussed the children, the weather, the juvenile judge and the cases they were working on while they ate.

They left the diner reluctantly, their meetings too brief to really cover everything in depth, but even that short hour of sharing helped relieve some of the pent-up worry, Caileen admitted as she hurried to her next appointment, which was with the gynecologist.

Jeff stood near the buffet table, a plate in one hand, a glass of wine in the other. He glanced around the elegant room, looking for a place to sit or at least put his drink down so he could eat.

At that moment Karen entered the huge, elegant

room with their hostess. She was striking in a green silky pantsuit. Her hair was swept away from her face on one side and held with a sparkling clasp.

"Attention, everyone," the owner called. "I want to introduce Karen Bennett, the designer responsible for our wonderful new home, and Jeff Aquilon, the artist who did all the outside artwork." The woman smiled at them. "Thank you both for making me so very happy with the décor and my husband happy with the budget."

Jeff felt like an idiot, standing there with a glass in one hand and a plate in the other while the crowd, all part of the elite homeowners in the area, laughed and applauded.

Karen handled the attention with aplomb. She nodded graciously to everyone and gave the homeowner a warm hug and an air-kiss. "Hi," she said to him when it was over. "Give me a minute and I'll join you."

He waited, glad that the spotlight had shifted. She filled a plate, grabbed a glass of champagne and led the way to the extended hearth of the fireplace. Flames danced over fake logs, creating a cozy ambiance. They sat at the end away from the heat and were silent while they ate.

"Sorry," Karen said when she finished. "I was starved. I didn't get time for lunch or dinner today." Glancing around, she added, "This is lovely, isn't it?"

"Yeah. The living room is bigger than my whole house."

"Not quite, but it is larger than my apartment. It's called the common area." Her sweeping gesture included all they could see. "This and the kitchen are part of the open plan that's popular nowadays."

He chuckled. "It's funny how things change. Kitchens used to be tucked in the back of the home and out of sight. Now they're part of the entertainment area."

Her tone was wry. "I would really be impressed if she'd used the kitchen to actually cook. The food was catered." She stood. "Well, this is a business evening for me. And for you—you know, the resident artist and all that. You should mingle. Or you can stand with an arm on the mantel and look dangerous when anyone approaches." She grinned and left.

Jeff recalled the arguments she'd used to get him there, money being the main one. With three kids, he figured he'd need a bundle for their education. Any money he earned from the sculptures went into that fund.

He gave his empty plate to a waiter, accepted another glass of wine and decided to study the artwork inside the mansion. A painting over the mantel had caught his eye.

"Interesting, isn't it?" a feminine voice asked.

He turned from the mountain scene to an attractive blonde who was perhaps in her late twenties. Her cocktail dress showed lots of cleavage.

"Yes. It looks like the mountains around here."

"It is. The artist is local, a recluse who prefers his own company. By the way, I'm Taylor."

She laughed in a manner that reminded him of Caileen's daughter when she was trying to flirt with him and explained that she was the niece of the homeowner and her father was president of the largest privately owned bank in the state.

Fifteen minutes later, Jeff stifled a yawn and checked the ornate clock on a side table.

"Do you have a headache or something?" his companion inquired. "You frowned," she added.

"Uh, just tired," he said, ashamed of being bored in light of her concern. "It's been a long week."

She gave him a sympathetic smile. "I know what you mean. My schedule has been simply hectic, one appointment after another. I handle all my father's entertaining."

"A big responsibility," he murmured.

It probably was. He didn't discount social activities as trivial. Karen wanted his work to become known so that the value of his sculptures would go up. That would please her clients and enhance her reputation as one who recognized up-and-coming talent. If he was smart, he'd grab onto the canny designer and let her make him rich.

The problem was, while he admired Karen's drive and common sense, he didn't want a partner. He could imagine her directing his entire life. That didn't fit his image of what a relationship should be.

Relationship? Hell, it wasn't as if he had the time to devote to a woman and all she would expect of a man.

Assuming any woman could get past his disability. After recovering from his wound, he'd soon discovered women reacted in one of two ways to his injury—they were either turned off by his lack of a foot or they were filled with pity and wanted to mother him. He didn't need either.

For some reason an image of Caileen came to mind. Her tears, her kisses, her passion had gotten to him in a way no woman had in years. She knew about his loss. He wondered if it would bother her. God, what was he thinking?

"I'm supposed to mingle. Anyone here you think I should meet?" he asked Taylor.

Her eyes lit up. This was clearly her bailiwick. "Come with me. I'll introduce you. I know everyone."

Amused, he let her lead him from one group to another while she beamed on him as if he was her protégé. After an hour, he thanked her for befriending him, told his hostess and Karen farewell and started on the long drive home.

It was nice drive, he reflected as peace descended over him now that he was alone. The night air was crisp but pleasant. The moon was nearly full. He liked the shadows of the night, as if the world had a coating of soot, all soft and black and fuzzy. By contrast, the moonlight cast the mountain peaks into stark detail, making them seem remote and cold but beautiful.

From inside him, unexpected emotion swirled. He slowed and made the turn into the driveway leading to his home. Up ahead, a light gleamed. The kids had left a welcoming lamp on for him. All that was needed was a sweet, loving woman to complete the picture of a perfect family.

He parked and turned off the engine, then sat there in bewilderment as emotion churned within. Something in him demanded attention. It wanted something from him.

He didn't have a clue as to what it was.

Chapter Six

Caileen gathered a bouquet of jonquils from the backyard and carried them to the patio table. She loved the colorful blooms, most of them in golden yellow, like bursts of sunlight captured in the petals.

She mixed them with the roses she'd already cut and together the blossoms created a flamboyant burst of color in the green vase. Going inside, she added more water and preservative, then set the container in the center of the table.

"Very pretty, Mom," Zia said, entering the kitchen.

She was still in her pajamas. Her hair was pulled back from her face with a scrunchy, making her look even younger than her nineteen years.

"Would you like some breakfast?" Caileen asked. "I was thinking of pancakes with blueberries."

"That would be super."

When the meal was ready, they went outside to eat. "It's warmer out here than in the house," Caileen remarked. "Look at the bees buzzing around."

Zia nodded and covered a yawn. "You worked late last night. Was there an emergency?"

"Only paperwork. Nan had her baby, so we have to cover for her while she's out on maternity leave," she explained about the marriage class.

"The last counselor didn't return after her baby was born. Do you think Nan will?"

Caileen sighed. "I sure hope so."

"Thirty-eight is old to be having kids."

"Well, a lot of women are waiting until later, it seems. Maybe raising children is easier when the parents are older and more confident of their skills."

"You were my age when you married," Zia pointed out. "I loved the early days with you and Dad. We had so much fun."

"Yes, we did," Caileen admitted. "Your father and I had as much growing up to do as you did." She laughed. "I can't believe we lived in a van for four years."

"You and Dad worked at everything from fruit picking to bagging groceries. That must have been a blast."

At her daughter's envious expression, Caileen sobered. "It was, but it was hard, too. Especially later. You needed a dust-free environment because of your asthma."

"So you found an apartment, finished your degree, got a permanent job and bought a house. How did you manage that?"

"I'd saved birthday money from my grandparents for years. Your father earned a lot in construction jobs, so I made sure we saved some of that. He always wanted to move on after a few months in one place, so I knew we would need it when we were on the road."

"Dad had to start from scratch when you divorced," Zia murmured, accusation in her tone.

Caileen swallowed the last bite of pancake with an effort. "I gave him exactly half of what we had saved together when he walked out."

"You told him to leave," Zia stated.

Caileen shook her head. She wasn't going to take this fall for Brendon. "He wanted to go. He didn't like being tied down to one place. I told him if he left he couldn't come back."

The old hurt of long ago rose in her heart, reminding her of the devastation of being abandoned and the fear of making it alone with a dependent child.

She took a deep breath and let it out slowly. Like a lot of women before her, she'd found she could survive on her own. But it had been hard.

"Your father had his dreams and I had mine," she said softly. "They didn't match at all. That's something you should think about."

Zia's expression turned stony. "If you're talking about me and Sammy, we don't have a problem."

Caileen gave her daughter a level stare. "Don't you? You're in the top ten percent of your class. Very smart. Very capable. Sammy's a dropout who couldn't manage to hold a C average—"

"School isn't his thing! He does a great job in construction. Like Dad. Just because things didn't work out for you two doesn't mean it will be the same for us," Zia interrupted. "*I* haven't dropped out of school to live in a van and go surfing."

"Good point," Caileen said. "I certainly don't want you making the same mistakes I did."

"Sammy isn't a mistake," Zia informed her.

Unfortunately, Caileen had observed Sammy closely in the six months he'd been seeing Zia. He was polite, good-looking...and used to getting by on charm. It must have come as a shock when his parents kicked him out.

She thought it was time for her daughter to also get a dose of reality. Taking a calming breath, she said, "He's a party guy who lives for the moment and his own pleasure. He expects you to adjust your schedule to his and he resents it when you don't."

Emotion flickered across Zia's face, and Caileen knew she'd hit a nerve. As a counselor, she also knew it didn't pay to argue with one's offspring. Instead, parents needed to set the rules of the house and insist that they be followed. If they weren't, then there had to be clearly defined consequences.

Zia knew she had to maintain decent grades; she had to help with household chores; she had to come and go at reasonable hours and keep Caileen informed of her plans, just as Caileen did with her. Otherwise she was free to get a job and her own place and live her life as she pleased.

As a mother, Caileen wanted so much more for her daughter than a dropout. "Sammy had his chance—and his parents' support—to make it through college. He wasted it. Don't let him waste yours, too."

"You sound like the school counselor." Resentment coated every word.

The statement rattled Caileen. Her tone was harsh when she asked, "Are you thinking of leaving school?"

Zia hesitated, then shook her head.

"Good. Get your education. That's the ticket to the freedom you want so much."

Silence stretched between them. Caileen was surprised that Zia didn't jump up and go to her room as she usually did when Sammy was the subject of discussion.

After a while, Caileen replenished her coffee and gazed at the vine-covered posts over the patio. "We need to redo the arbor. The paint is peeling."

Zia shrugged.

Caileen continued. "It's been ten years since we put the arbor together from a kit. Some of the posts are loose. Remember how we agonized over what colors to use for the paint?"

"Yes, and settled on green and white so they wouldn't clash with the flowers we planned to use."

"Then we had to select the plants."

Zia nodded, her mood becoming reminiscent. "I wanted to order one of everything. The flowers in the seed catalogs were so beautiful, I couldn't decide between them."

"We learned by trial and error—"

"A lot of error," Zia said with a certain ruefulness.

"Yes, but we did learn." Caileen wanted to use the example of the flowers to segue into a lesson on choosing wisely, but she decided not to further push the thorny subject of boyfriends versus life partners. She'd made her views known. Now Zia needed time for reflection.

Zia left with Sammy at midmorning to go to a spring fair—a fund-raiser for school supplies—at a nearby Native American reservation. Caileen finished her chores, ate lunch, read for a while, then, restless, decided to head for the Aquilon homestead for advice.

Caileen parked her car near the flagstone walk at the Aquilon place. The three young people stopped weeding the garden and perused her with obvious wariness in their expressions.

"Hello," she called, including all of them in her glance and the smile meant to put them at ease.

"Hello," Jeremy replied, rising from the flower bed beside the walkway and stepping toward her as if to place his physical presence between her and the children.

An instinctive move on his part, she observed. "Is your uncle available?"

"He's working in the shop." Jeremy gestured toward the building. "Go on down."

"Thank you. It's a lovely day to be outside, isn't it?" she said to Krista, pausing beside the girl.

Krista nodded and, to Caileen's surprise, fell into step beside her. "Uncle Jeff told me what you said about the other girls at school. Monday I'm going to invite them to play kickball with me and my friends."

"I hope that tactic works," Caileen said.

"Me, too. There's Uncle Jeff," Krista said, smiling and waving. "He's working on a new sculpture." She stepped off the path and started weeding around the birdbath.

Feeling self-conscious as Jeff waited for her at the open door to the workshop, Caileen continued along the path.

"A surprise inspection?" he asked when she drew near, his gaze wary.

She shook her head. "I'm looking for tips on home maintenance."

His dark eyebrows rose slightly at her announcement, but he took the news in stride. "Sure. Have a seat. I'm working on something, but I can talk while I work."

She sat on a high stool and watched as he slipped

a metal spiral over a piece of copper tubing. He began shaping the copper into a long smooth curve, his hands moving slowly and patiently as he bent the piece.

He wore shorts and a T-shirt today since it was warm. His socks were scrunched at his ankles, just above a pair of well-worn sneakers. Staring at the flesh-toned material of the artificial foot, she imagined the pain he must have gone through when the mine blew up.

"Does it bother you?" he asked, his eyes following her line of sight.

The very calmness in his voice told her there'd been others who *had* been bothered by the prosthetic.

"No." She met his hard gaze without flinching. "I was wondering if it hurt…when it happened."

"I was conscious until I was brought to the medical station and given a shot. Oddly, the pain wasn't as bad then as after the surgery. I guess I was in shock."

"You've adjusted very well."

He shrugged. "I've had a few years to get used to the idea. Losing a foot didn't interfere with my work. If I'd lost a hand, I'm not sure how I would feel."

Pausing, he held his hands up and studied them as if trying to imagine living without one.

"You would make it just fine," she said, realizing she was very sure of this fact.

"Would I now?" he drawled.

Going back to his work, he gave her a smile. She

realized he was pleased at her prognosis. A sweet feeling settled in the pit of her stomach.

Don't, she warned herself. Those kinds of feelings got a person in trouble. She never wanted to be vulnerable that way again.

"What problems are you having with home maintenance?" he asked, bringing them back to the point of her visit.

"Well, the arbor over the back patio is ten years old. Besides needing paint, it's leaning to the right a bit. I'm not sure how to brace it. Also, what do I do with the vines growing on it while I paint?"

He bent to one side as he held the copper pipe against others he'd already welded together. The muscles in his back rippled under the faded blue of the cotton knit.

She thought of his strength, then of his tenderness as he held her while she'd wept all over him the previous week.

Recalling their kisses, she admitted she'd wanted much more from him than comfort. It had been a long time since she'd shared any kind of intimacy with a man. When he'd kissed her, she'd gone from the warmth of his concern to the sizzle of passion in an instant.

For someone who prided herself on maintaining control, that had been a mind-boggling experience when she'd later thought it over. Yes, she'd forgiven herself for the slip, but that hadn't erased the memory of his touch….

She sighed.

"Any other problems?" he asked, glancing up from his work.

"Nothing major. Krista said you were doing a new sculpture. Is that it?"

He nodded. "It's a commission for the plaza of the new bank going up in town, so I'll get paid for it."

She returned his wry smile. "How nice."

"About your arbor," he said, "I can come by later this afternoon to take a look and maybe give you some helpful hints."

She realized she'd again gotten off the subject. "Thank you."

His eyes met hers. A funny ripple dashed around inside her. Flustered, she looked away and asked, "Uh, does it bother you if someone watches while you work?"

"Not as a rule. You can stay as long as you want."

Thirty minutes passed in almost total silence. Absorbed by his skill, she didn't notice the time. "You like to work in copper, don't you?" she finally said when he finished the piece he'd been working on. It formed part of a long skirt on a woman.

"Yes. I decided to make it my specialty. I like the feel of it and the way it weathers when left outside." He stood back and peered at the form from every angle. "She's a pioneer," he explained. "The banker's ancestors came here by train after the civil war. He wanted to commemorate them and the efforts of the first settlers."

"They probably displaced some of your ancestors," she murmured, recalling there was Native American blood on his mother's side of the family, according to his personal record, while his father came from English and Mexican stock. "Doesn't that bother you?"

"No. Nothing I do now can change the past, so there's no point in dwelling on it."

"A wise decision."

"The same goes for you." He took a drink from a tall insulated mug, then held it out to her. "Iced tea."

She accepted the tacit invitation and took a sip. It was flavored with raspberry. "Very good." She handed the mug back to him.

He studied her while he drank again.

"What did you mean—the same goes for me?" she asked when he set the drink aside.

"I think you're stuck in the past. You're afraid your daughter is going to repeat your mistakes."

For some reason she thought of her first night alone, the night her husband had walked out and left her with the bills and a four-year-old.

A thunderstorm had rolled down the mountain that long-ago night, bringing rain and hail and zigzags of lightning that had ripped the sky to shreds. The old apartment building at the university had groaned and swayed in the wind. Water had blown in around the loose windows. She'd never been so frightened in her life.

"I see her with Sammy, all starry-eyed and trusting and...and it's me all over again."

"That's tough. You want to force-feed your lessons to the next generation, but they want to learn from their own experiences and observations." He paused, then asked, "How long were your parents married before you were born?"

It took a second to grasp the meaning of his question. "Five months," she said. "It wasn't until I was expecting Zia that my mother told me. My parents never celebrated their wedding anniversary, so I didn't realize they had to get married."

"Maybe that's why they were so harsh when you dropped out of school and took off with your lover. They didn't want you to repeat their mistake."

"I wasn't pregnant when Brendon and I married." She sounded a bit indignant when she related this information.

"But you were soon afterward. You dropped out of college and lived in a van. I'm sure they viewed it as ruining your life."

"The way theirs was ruined when they married," she murmured, more to herself than him. "Mother postponed her counseling degree and worked while my father finished getting his accounting credentials. I was in elementary school before she returned to her studies."

"So they punished you for repeating their error. Are you going to pass that along to Zia if she does the same?"

Caileen stared at him in despair. "It was so hard back then. Zia had asthma. She needed a dust-free environment. I worked two jobs and went to school…."

She stopped and inhaled deeply, ashamed that she'd disclosed this much.

"It's okay to grieve," he said. "It's necessary in order to go on. But first you have to forgive yourself for being young and foolish and in love."

"I have. I got over it."

"Did you?" He gazed into her eyes for a long moment. "You can tell Zia your worries and about the past, but then, I think you have to let her choose her own fate."

She tried to smile, but inside she felt too sad. "I know that. In my mind I know it, but in my heart I would give anything to save her pain."

"Mothers are like that," he said.

She knew he was thinking of his own past. His mother hadn't chosen wisely in her mate, but she'd apparently been loving to her children. But sometimes, she mused sadly, it took more than love to save a child from heartbreak. She just didn't know what it was.

"I'll see you later today," he promised.

She nodded. "Thank you."

Driving home, she wasn't sure what she was the most grateful for—his advice on Zia, his agreement to check the arbor or his patience whenever she brought her problems to him. He was a good listener, but, as she reminded herself sternly, that was supposed to be her job.

* * *

Jeff arrived at the attractive cottage shortly after four. He'd showered and changed to khaki slacks and a white shirt.

"Hello," a feminine voice called.

He got out of the pickup and looked around.

"Over here."

Caileen stood under a climbing rose that sprawled over a trellis. She was pruning the canes before the rose smothered the clematis that was growing on the same support.

His heart knocked against his ribs as he crossed the neatly trimmed lawn and stood beside her. He didn't know if it was her or the roses he smelled but the scent was heady.

She wore faded jeans, a large T-shirt in bright gold and jogging shoes. A sun visor shaded her eyes and kept her hair off her face. She looked young and happy.

"You like working with plants," he said, noting the wheelbarrow filled with pruned branches.

"They don't talk back."

He liked the snappy comeback and the cheery tone of delivery. She wasn't as tense as she'd been earlier.

"Thanks for coming over. I hope you didn't stop your work prematurely on my account. There's no hurry on the arbor."

When she placed her gloves and gardening shears in the wheelbarrow, he lifted the handles. "Where do you want this?" he asked.

"Around back. This way."

He followed her to the backyard and the compost heap enclosed in a circle of stock fence. He observed as she lifted the debris with a pitchfork and tossed it on a fresh pile of grass clippings. "You've been busy today."

She smiled in a carefree manner that started his heart to knocking again. "On weekends I can't wait until the neighbors are up and about so I can start the yard work. I think of it as therapy."

"Making things in the shop does the same for me."

"I made a fresh pitcher of sangria. Would you like some?" she asked, leading the way to the back patio.

"Sounds great."

He tried not to think about being here with her the previous weekend, but sexual tension hummed along every nerve in his body as he sat in a cushioned patio chair and studied the structure of the arbor.

"You did a good job putting this together," he complimented her when she handed him a tall glass of fruit juice mixed with white wine.

"The posts are sort of shaky. I don't want it to fall down, especially on a guest."

Leaning forward, he pushed against one of the support posts. "Mmm," he said. "Definitely shaky."

He removed the all-purpose knife from his pocket, selected the screwdriver and poked the bottom of the post. The tip went through the wood as if it were a sponge.

"I know that isn't a good sign," she said.

Noting the anxiety in her expression, he hated to tell her the news. Before declaring a disaster, he checked each wooden section of the arbor carefully.

"Well," he said, "it isn't as bad as it could be."

Giving a fatalistic smile, she asked, "How bad is it?"

"Some of the posts have rotted off at the base, but the rest of the structure is sound."

"That's treated lumber," she protested. "It isn't supposed to rot. It was guaranteed for twenty years."

"When you cut off the ends of the posts to fit under the eaves, you cut off the treated part. You needed to use wood preservative and sealer on each cut piece."

"The instructions didn't mention that."

He smiled at the indignant statement. "Yeah, they probably assume homeowners know what they're doing."

She pursed her lips in disgust. "That's stupid."

"Right."

Keeping his expression neutral, he met her gaze. When she grinned, he did, too.

"Okay, I'm the stupid one." She sighed loudly. "What do I do now?"

"Replace the supports. I doubt they'll hold up in a heavy winter snow."

"How much do you think it'll cost?"

"Around a thousand dollars."

When she puckered up in dismay, he fought a

mixture of emotion that had him torn between galloping to the rescue and volunteering to fix the patio, or kissing her until the sticker shock left her eyes.

"If you hire it out," he continued when she was silent. "If you do it yourself, you're talking about ten posts at twenty bucks each. Two hundred dollars."

"Zia and I built this from a kit. It was on sale for five hundred dollars. We were so proud when we did it."

She touched one of the posts as if caressing a lifelong friend, her gesture one of farewell.

Before he knew quite what he was going to say, he found himself coming to her aid. "It's a simple job. We can do it in an afternoon."

"We?" she questioned, glancing around as if wondering if someone else had materialized on the patio.

"Sure. I'll help. All we need to do is prop up the cross pieces, remove the old post and put in a new one." He inspected the arbor once more. "Since it needs painting, we can cut back the vines—they're getting pretty woody anyway—and let them get a fresh start. I'm surprised the roses have lasted this long."

"I don't think I can allow you to help," she said in her serious manner that he found endearing for some reason. "I'm counselor for the children under your care."

"And therefore we're a team working toward the same goal," he reminded her. "You're supposed to help me guide the kids on the right path. I don't see why I can't help you with one of your projects since it falls within my area of expertise."

Her chest rose and fell in a deep breath while she thought it over. "Are you sure you don't mind? I can get a neighbor to help."

He shook his head. "You want to get started tomorrow? We can go to the lumberyard and pick up the posts, also some bags of cement to set them in. That way, they'll stand up to summer thunderstorms and winter blizzards."

Her smile was unexpected, a gift like Krista's birthday kiss. And like the child's show of affection, it warmed his heart in a strange, new and tender way.

Watch it, he warned, but he didn't know what he was guarding himself against. He searched his brain for a neutral subject. "Jeremy's taking the kids to a movie tonight. Both did super on major tests this week, so he volunteered to give them a treat."

"That was nice of him." Her eyes darkened. "Zia is with Sammy."

Jeff observed the emotion that flickered over her face at the mention of her daughter. If he had a kid with Zia's looks, he would probably worry a lot, too. "I'm glad I have a few more years before I have to start worrying about Krista and boys."

Caileen gave him an envious stare. "I think Jeremy and Tony will look after her interests. You won't have to do a thing."

"That's a relief." He lifted his glass in a salute of one parent to another. It occurred to him that if they combined households, Jeremy could keep an eye on Zia as well as Krista.

For a second he was astounded at the idea. He didn't know where it had come from, what evil fairy had waved her magic wand and planted an impossible thought in his brain.

"I have chips and a roasted pepper dip. Would you like some?" Caileen asked.

He nodded and sipped the refreshing fruit drink, which helped cool his head. The problem was the sensual hunger that burned through him whenever he was around Caileen.

Or thought about her.

Muttering an imprecation, he wondered why this had to happen now that his life was settled once more. He had everything he needed or wanted. Well, almost.

His bed was empty and had been for five years. So what else was new?

Maybe that was the problem—his other worries were over, so his libido had kicked in again. Yeah, that was it. The attractive counselor had just happened into his life at the right moment...or the wrong moment.

He shook his head at his ridiculous ruminations, then smiled when Caileen returned, carrying a tray with some tantalizing snacks. His stomach rumbled. He realized he was hungry, but for food this time.

"That looks good," he said.

"I have some French onion dip in case the roasted pepper one is awful. It's from a recipe I saw in a magazine the other day."

"You like to cook?"

She considered his question, pursing up her lips in that interesting way she had. "I like to try new things," she finally decided. "New foods, new plants in the garden, a different arrangement of furniture."

"You're adventurous," he accused, liking the image this produced.

"No way. I get panicky if things are out of control. I'm the serious and somber type."

"According to Zia. That's not how I see you."

Her eyebrows rose at this declaration. "How do you see me?"

He swished a carrot into the pepper dip and tasted it. "Umm, spicy and delicious," he murmured, partially closing his eyes as he looked at her. He was pretty sure he was playing with fire. Ask him if he cared.

For months—years—he'd been cautious about involvement. He hadn't let anyone get too close. Suddenly he wanted closeness…intimacy…touching…

"Don't," she said hoarsely.

"Don't what?"

"Look at me that way."

"What way?"

"Like I'm Red Riding Hood and you're the wolf."

Her husky laughter was shaky, and he was pretty sure she knew exactly what he was thinking. He finished off the carrot and took a long drink of sangria. It didn't cool his fevered thoughts one degree.

"That's what I feel," he admitted, then laughed. If he could joke about it, he could control the impulse.

Maybe.

When she looked directly into his eyes, he was pretty sure he couldn't.

"Hell," he said and reached for her.

"We shouldn't," she said, but she fitted nicely in his arms. "We can't get involved. We have to think of the children, not…not mad passion."

"I like thinking about mad passion," he murmured, kissing the spot under her right ear that was so damn tantalizing.

She laid her hands against his chest as if to hold him off, then caressed him with her fingers, sending fire through him. He was pretty sure she didn't even realize what she was doing, how instinctively sensual she was.

He suddenly wished he'd met her first, long before her dreams were smashed on the rocks of reality, back when she was eager for adventure and he…he was still a whole man….

Dream on.

Gazing into her troubled eyes, he dropped his arms and stepped back. "What time to you want to pick up the new posts tomorrow?"

Chapter Seven

Caileen woke as the sun rose over the tree-lined ridge east of the house and spilled brilliant spring light into her bedroom window. Tossing back the covers, she leaped from the bed as if she had an urgent appointment, then took twice as long as usual to make up her mind about what to wear that day.

"Silly," she muttered to herself. As if it mattered which jeans and T-shirt she wore. This was not a date.

Restless after breakfast, she wrote up the case file notes on her laptop while her daughter and the neighbors slept late. Caught up on both yard and house chores, she had nothing pressing to do until she and Jeff went shopping for the new posts.

A funny tingle ran down her neck and lodged in

her breasts as she thought of him. Never in fifteen years of singledom had she allowed herself to have an affair just because she was attracted to a man in the most physical way she'd ever experienced.

Other than when she'd first fallen for Brendon, she added in total honesty. At nineteen she'd thought intense physical attraction was the same as everlasting love.

Seven years ago she'd thought mutual interests and respect were enough to ensure a lasting relationship, but after two years of trying to convince herself they were in love, she and the college professor had decided they were destined to be friends.

And they were still friendly whenever they happened to meet. So were his wife and two kids.

At ten she heard Zia stir. When her daughter came into the kitchen, Caileen gave the girl a quick once-over.

In jeans and a blue shirt over a stretchy white top, neither of which quite managed to cover her belly button, and with only a tiny red scar on the side of the neck, Zia was a lovely specimen of health and youthful energy.

"What are your plans for the day?" Caileen asked.

"Library first. Is it okay if I take the car?"

"Yes, I won't need it."

"Sammy and I are going to a, mmm, party later this afternoon. It's a barbecue, so I won't be in for dinner. I'll drop the car off before we go."

Caileen wondered if the outing was really a keg

party. Suppressing additional questions, she smiled and said, “Have a good time.”

Zia hesitated as she poured milk over a bowl of cereal. “What are you going to do?”

“Jeff Aquilon is coming over. We’re going to get new posts for the arbor and, I hope, replace the old ones this afternoon.”

“Are you dating?” Zia asked bluntly, disapproval clearly written all over her face.

A jolt went through Caileen. “Hardly. I asked for his advice. He volunteered to help.”

“I see.”

Caileen maintained a neutral expression. She didn’t have to ask her daughter’s permission to date. Not that she was dating, but if she ever did…

Oh, forget it, she advised as her thoughts became a jumble of excuses and explanations for this outing.

After Zia left for the library, Caileen made another pot of coffee, then decided to bake a pan of brownies for Jeff and his family.

An hour later she removed two pans from the oven. She’d made one pan with walnuts in the mixture, then realizing that everyone might not like the nutty flavor, she’d made another batch without.

At exactly one o’clock, Jeff pulled into the driveway. Posts protruded from the truck bed. She went outside.

“Hi,” he said, joining her beside the pickup. “I ran across a bargain in posts and snapped them up. I hope you don’t mind.”

“No. Where did you find them?”

While he explained about an order being cut too short at the local ranch-supply store, she helped unload the six-by-six posts and stack them beside the patio.

"Hey, the vines are gone," he noted.

"I cut them back yesterday afternoon as you suggested. The first cut was the hardest," she admitted. "It took ten years to grow them."

"They'll shoot back up in no time." He held up a cement block. "These are concrete piers. They'll anchor the new posts and keep them off the ground," he said when she stared at them somewhat perplexed as he unloaded the other nine. "I got ready-mix, too. And rented a posthole digger."

"Uh, how much do I owe you for all this?" She figured five hundred dollars out of the roofing fund.

He reached into his shirt pocket and handed her the itemized bill. She frowned as she checked off each item and realized the bill included everything. "This is less than two hundred dollars."

"I told you—the posts were a bargain."

His pleased grin made him look younger. Her insides did a strange flip. She was very aware that he was a man, one who was handsome, skilled and very much in his prime.

"I had some wood preservative, so the ends are treated for insects and fungus. I also used a water sealer on them. These posts will last twenty, thirty years."

"I think I've put you to a lot of trouble," she murmured, her misgivings about the wisdom of working together returning. Being near him gave her quivery feelings and ideas. Lots of ideas.

His sharp glance stifled the words.

"But I really appreciate your help," she finished. "Thank you very much."

His smile returned, and she suddenly felt much better about the whole thing. He stripped off the long-sleeved shirt and tossed it in the cab of the pickup. She noted the movement of muscle and sinew beneath the thin cotton of an old T-shirt.

A hot flush spread over her entire body while her fingers tingled as if electricity poured through them. She knew how strong he was, how smoothly the muscles rippled under his skin…

"Ready?" he asked. "Let's get with it," he said after she nodded.

With little conversation, they emptied the truck and set up a workstation in the backyard. At his instruction she learned how to brace the joists of the arbor with two-by-fours so they could remove the rotted post.

The posthole digger was gasoline powered and made short work of preparing new holes. He showed her how to pour in the ready-mix, add water and set in the concrete anchors.

On top of those, they installed the new support posts and attached them to the cross beams by nailing them in at an angle, a process he called "toe-nailing."

As they worked, their hands, arms and shoulders brushed each other in casual strokes. Hot quivers coursed through her at the slightest touch. She set her mind on the task at hand and managed for whole moments to ignore the clamoring of her body for more intimate gestures.

Halfway through the task, they took a break. She served iced tea and a plate of brownies. Coming out the back door, she saw he'd stripped off the T-shirt. He wiped the sweat from his face and tossed the shirt over a chair.

She nearly fell over her own feet as she stared at his muscular torso. A thick bed of hair covered his chest. She immediately had a vision of laying her head there and feeling secure and cherished.

With an effort, she forced the image, along with a surge of hunger, to subside. It would probably be a terrible faux pas to attack a guest in her home and demand that he make wild, passionate love to her when he was just trying to be helpful, she reminded her libido.

But it was tempting.

"Hey, those look good," he said, taking a seat at the patio table.

She set the plate on the table. "Help yourself."

To me, she thought, and was immediately on guard, afraid he would sense the lust raging in her, that he could see it in her eyes, this wanton desire that had no place in the grand scheme of arbor repair. Or her life.

When she glared at him, he raised his eyebrows and gave her a questioning stare.

"The brownies on this side of the plate have nuts," she said. "The others don't. I fixed some for you to take home to the kids, too."

"Thanks."

Her face felt hot as he studied her with a sardonic expression in his dark eyes. She was sure he knew of the turmoil he caused inside her. It wasn't funny, and she wanted to tell him so, but since neither of them was acknowledging the problem, she would keep her muddled thoughts to herself—

Oh, shut up.

Good advice.

Zia returned while they were still seated. She beamed at Jeff, confiscated several brownies and left with Sammy after telling her mom not to wait up.

Caileen listened to the fading sound of Sammy's pickup and wondered if she should be concerned about her daughter's safety. It had only been eight days since she'd been hurt.

"Ready to get back to work?" Jeff asked.

She nodded and rose.

"It doesn't do any good to worry," he said.

"I know."

"But you do it anyway. So do I, and I'm only a quasi-parent or something like that."

His laughter was gentle, and it soothed her heart. "I think she's outgrowing Sammy. In fact, she might have a crush on you." She gave him a quick glance to see how he took this information.

"Well, you don't have to worry about me taking her to any drag races or wild parties. Zia would definitely place me in the boring category after one outing."

His tone was that of one parent to another. It

added another layer of intimacy, of shared experience, between them. Heaven help her, but she'd never wanted a man as much as she did this one!

They finished the last post as twilight brushed sooty shadows over the land and the last rays of the sun turned the snow on the western peaks into a fiery glow.

"I can't believe we're done," she said, admiring their handiwork. "It took me and Zia a month to put it up."

She gave each post a test shake and found them all firm to the touch. Laughing in delight, she turned to him.

His smile as he watched her made her breath catch. It dipped right down inside her, stirring all those secret places of unrest and longing that had plagued her all afternoon. They stared at each other for an eternity.

"It's late," she finally said. "I have steaks in the freezer. Can you stay and have dinner?"

He nodded. "I told the kids I didn't know how long this would take. Krista made a pot of soup from a recipe in my mother's cookbook, so they're okay for dinner."

No longer working, Caileen shivered in the cooling night air. "Well, then, shall we go in?"

"Where do you want the old posts? I'll stack them out of the way for you."

"Beside the garden shed. Is any part of them usable?" she asked, carrying one end of a post and leading the way.

"Sure. Cut off the rotten end and seal the wood.

They'll make good fence posts if you need to replace any."

"I was thinking of a raised bed for a vegetable garden. I've been wanting to try one for a long time."

"That should work," he said in approval. "Raised beds provide good drainage."

She helped him load the posthole digger into the pickup. He tossed his T-shirt into the cab and retrieved the other shirt, then asked, "Where can I wash up?"

"Uh, there's a bathroom down the hall and on the left. You can shower if you want to. There're towels in the cabinet beside the bathtub."

He nodded and followed her into the house, then continued down the hall after placing his work shoes next to the door. In a moment she heard the shower come on. The sound came with mental pictures that caused her heartbeat to surge. She groaned under her breath.

Using the microwave, she thawed two steaks and left them in a bowl of marinade before going to her room. There she slipped out of her dusty clothing and took the quickest shower and shampoo in history.

After blow-drying, she pushed the hair off her face with a stretchy band and dressed in green sweatpants and a matching top that looked good on her.

Not that she was trying to catch Jeff's eye. She wasn't. At least, not purposefully. Although he was very attractive. "Arghhh," she muttered and stomped out.

Back in the kitchen, she wrapped two ears of corn

in wet paper towels and stuck them in the microwave to cook while she made a salad.

Jeff returned, dressed in jeans and a long-sleeved shirt, which was rolled back on his forearms and open a couple of buttons along the front.

Placing rolls in the toaster oven, she frowned at the fast beating of her heart and the way tingles rolled over her in waves of anticipation. Really, she had to get herself under control, or else her guest might think…

She paused to consider.

"Shall I start the steaks?" he asked, breaking into her ruminations.

"Oh, yes, please." She pointed to the platter she'd set on the counter near the door. After setting the table, she opened a bottle of red wine and placed it and two red-stemmed wineglasses beside the plates.

The glasses had been a wedding gift from a high school friend twenty-one years ago. So long and yet such a short time, she mused, a tinge of sadness creeping in and altering the exhilaration of finishing the arbor project.

When Jeff brought the steaks in, he took a chair next to where she always sat rather than at the end of the table.

"I've had the wine for a long time," she told him. "You'd better check to see if it's drinkable."

He poured a sip and tasted it. "Perfect. A very good vintage, I'm sure," he said, laughing. He filled each glass and raised his. "To a job well done."

She touched her glass to his. "Very well done," she agreed. "I can't thank you enough."

Looking into each other's eyes, they drank the wine. Time shifted. A moment became forever, eternity the space between two heartbeats.

She felt dizzy, achy…happy…uncertain.

"Eat," he said quite gently.

That brought her back to earth. She put the glass down and picked up her fork.

"That was delicious," Jeff said after eating every last morsel on his plate. A sense of contentment stole over him. Seeing that Caileen was also finished, he refilled their wineglasses. "Shall we sit outside and enjoy the arbor?"

She nodded. "Would you like a brownie for dessert?"

"Not now. Maybe later."

When he rose, she did, too. He opened the back door and stood aside to let her exit first. She stopped on the threshold. She seemed about to say more but stayed silent, her eyes going darker as she gazed up at him. She blinked, turned and walked out onto the patio.

He ignored the harsh, demanding rush of testosterone through his body and closed the door behind them.

Outside, the twilight had deepened to dusky darkness and a half moon floated lazily in the sky. Protected from the evening breeze by the house, the patio offered a restful retreat. He settled in a cushioned chair next to her. The scent of flowers filled the space around them.

"It's odd to see the stars so clearly. I'm used to the roses covering the arbor and obscuring them," she said.

He felt a bit strange himself. A quiet watchfulness came over him. He felt at peace with the world, yet a hum of expectation sang through him.

Glancing at his companion when she sighed—she had her head resting on the chair and was studying the sky—he admitted it wasn't so odd. He was deeply aware of her…and knew that she was the same with him. He chuckled.

"What?" she asked in a lazy tone.

"It's like being in high school again and having a crush on a girl. You know where she is all the time. Your body tingles when she's near. Your eyes are drawn to her and hers to you. It's funny and awful at the same time."

Rolling her head to the side, she gazed at him very seriously. "We're not in high school."

"Thank God. I wouldn't want to go through growing up all over again. Would you?"

She shook her head. The dim light shining through the curtained kitchen window reflected in her eyes as she stared at him with a thoughtful frown. "Do we ever really grow up? Sometimes I feel as uncertain as I did then."

A sleepy cricket whirred near them. He listened to the lonely call for a minute before saying, "People never stop planning and dreaming. We're always rushing ahead, bent on reaching some elusive goal."

"What is your goal, Jeff?"

He shrugged. "I don't know."

"Or won't say," she accused but in a gentle humor. "Men always avoid such subjects."

He inhaled and released a deep breath. "Okay, you asked for this," he told her. "You. I want you."

The stillness changed in an instant, yet he didn't regret his words. He held her gaze for a long moment before she looked away. She sat up, and he did regret the tension evident in the set of her shoulders.

"I shouldn't have said that," he began.

"Don't apologize. I asked for it." She pressed a hand to the frown now on her forehead. "We're adults. We can admit to an attraction...and control our impulses."

He suppressed a smile as she very seriously tried to be candid about the situation, admitting the need but making it clear they weren't going to act on it.

"I'm not too sure about that. I've been having erotic thoughts about you all day."

"Really," she said.

A reprimand.

"Really," he said.

When she glared at him, he couldn't keep from grinning, inviting her to share the irony of wanting the one person each of them shouldn't become involved with.

"This is ridiculous," she told him.

"You're absolutely right."

"Impossible."

"Right again."

"Unwise." She covered her eyes with her hands.

"I think I'll die if you don't kiss me," she said in a whisper.

"Same here."

He leaned forward and lifted her from the chair and into his lap. The patio chair squeaked loudly.

"Uh, I suggest we adjourn to the sofa." He rose and set her on her feet. "We should be able to make out without falling on our butts there."

He chuckled as her eyes widened. He expected a refusal, but she nodded and led the way inside. He caught her hand in one of his and flicked off the kitchen light with the other.

"Now," he said and knew this was what he'd been wanting from the moment he'd arrived.

She met the kiss without hesitation. Their bodies melded as if made for one another when she arched upward on her toes and wrapped her arms around his shoulders.

It was magic and enchantment. He was spellbound by the sweet womanly warmth of her, the wonderful scent that filled his nostrils, the just-right feel of her body against his.

He let his hands roam her back, her hips, along her sides. Pausing, he cupped his thumbs under her breasts, then slid them gently upward, gliding between their bodies so that he could sweep over the hardened tips.

His body went to red alert as hunger pushed every thought but fulfillment from his mind. When she gave a little moan and moved against his hands, he thought he just might explode as his blood rapidly reached boiling.

Raising his head and lifting her so that her feet cleared the floor, he went into the dark living room and found the sofa without mishap.

Dropping into its comfortable cushions, he half lay against the corner. Using his toes, he flicked the fleecy slippers from her feet and rolled to his side, settling her between his body and the sofa back. When he pressed with his knee, she opened her thighs so that their legs meshed into a sensual tangle.

Their mouths met and fire danced between them, over them, through them, as they shared the heated stirring of passion. He felt like a teenager again, ravenous and reckless as only the young and inexperienced could be.

The hell of it was that he didn't care.

When he slid a hand under her fleece-lined top, he discovered smooth flesh. No bra or other clothing impeded the exploration of her delectable body. Her breast filled his hand to perfection, the tip pressing hard into his palm as she rose to meet his touch.

Her little murmurs and gasps of pleasure fed the passionate delight. Her light touches over his shoulders and neck urged him on. When she slipped the shirt buttons free and buried her face against his chest, he closed his eyes against the whirl of emotions that rushed through him.

Protective. Possessive. Tender. Fierce.

Caileen reacted instinctively, in ways she'd

thought she'd forgotten. Now, sensations flooded into her body and mind, drowning the voices of caution that had ruled her every waking moment for years.

She gave herself to the passion, to the sharing of intimacy like a child at a favorite playground, going from one exciting thing to the next. His kisses were hot cotton candy, and she stuffed herself on them. They dueled with their tongues, then made up with delicious little touches and licks.

When they broke the kiss in order to breathe, she pressed her nose into the cushiony chest hair and kissed him a thousand times. She laughed as his nipples hardened under the caress of her mouth.

With the pure abandon that comes from freedom, she moved against him, gasping at the quick, hot infusion of hunger the sensual stroking produced.

When his hand glided downward, she held her breath. The stretchy waistband of her sweatpants was no barrier. A primal force grew in her as he paused, then continued the journey of exploration.

"Jeff," she said, unable to keep the demand, the plea, locked inside. "I want…"

"What? Tell me," he invited, his voice husky and sexy and low.

"You. Just…you."

Jeff tried to draw air into his lungs, but it was like breathing underwater. He couldn't get enough oxygen to dispel the mistiness that clouded his brain. Hell, he didn't even want to.

He wanted the hot, mindless sex his body

demanded and the boundless intimacy she unconsciously invited with her cries and movements, all urging them to completion.

There were other feelings swirling in the mists but he didn't try to sort them out. It was enough to hold her, to touch her this way, to find her ready for him and as demanding in her need as he was. For now, this was enough.

When she tugged at the snap on his waistband, he eased away and sat up. "Wait," he murmured.

Caileen contained her impatience as an odd sort of tenderness spread through her. The way his hands shook slightly as he removed jeans and briefs, then tossed the shirt aside, was endearing.

He paused at the fastening of the artificial foot, his manner once again wary. She instinctively knew some woman had hurt him when he was the most vulnerable to his loss. Anger at that woman filled her. Bending forward, she said, "Let me."

Quickly and without hesitation, she finished the task of removing the metal and plastic, then placed it under the coffee table, out of the way but within reach. She glanced casually at his left leg, then smiled at him, an invitation to proceed.

The slight awkwardness as he retrieved a condom from his pocket spoke of needs long unmet. That he was careful and considerate as he helped her with her clothes told her more about him than the fifty-page file in her office could ever convey.

She smiled at the trembling of her own fingers

as they removed her clothing, glad that she hadn't taken the time to put on underwear. It would only be in the way.

When he turned to her, she was ready. She lifted her arms and invited him in. He came eagerly, urgently to her, but also slowly, giving her time to adjust to his fullness.

"It's been a long time for me, too," he murmured when they were fully joined. "Are you all right?"

"Perfect," she said.

They smiled at each other, then he bent to her mouth once more. They kissed and touched for a long time. When her cries became impatient he acceded to the demands of the hunger between them.

Sated they came to rest, contented, neither wanting to move for an eternity.

Caileen sighed.

He raised his head and peered at her, concern in his eyes. She felt the pressure of tears and refused to let them fall. After such bliss, what was there to cry about?

"I have to go," he said and now there was regret in his tone, plus a wry acknowledgment of other responsibilities.

"I know." She stroked his firm jaw, liking the rasp of his beard against her palm. "Your family will be expecting you."

"I want to stay. It's been a long time since I've felt this way. I want it to last."

But even as he spoke, he was rising, finding his clothing, slipping into it and the parental role he'd taken on. When he replaced the prosthesis, she realized she hadn't once noticed the absence of a foot, she'd been that lost in his wonderful embrace.

Finished, he paused and studied her as if he wanted to ask her something. Instead, he smiled and stood.

An echo of the earlier anger on his behalf reverberated through her. "Everything was simply wonderful," she murmured fiercely, a tigress in full defensive mode. "I don't want it to end, either."

She pulled on her sweats and went with him to the kitchen door, flipped on the light while he tugged on his shoes, then went outside with him as he left. She lifted her face for his kiss just as a car pulled into the drive. Its lights brightly illuminated the yard and the arbor, bare of its concealing vines.

"Damn," he said as Zia got out and came toward them in a near run.

"Go on," she told him. "I'll handle this. Zia and I need a little private time."

When he gave her a worried glance, she pushed on his shoulder to speed him along. He squeezed her hand, said good night to Zia as they passed and left the daughter standing at one end of the patio glaring at her mother.

Chapter Eight

"*What* is going on?" Zia demanded.

Caileen closed and locked the door behind them. The kitchen clock indicated it was a few minutes after midnight.

A new day, she noted, and resisted the guilty anger parents feel when questioned by their children.

"Between you and Jeff," Zia continued.

Caileen managed a smile. "We replaced the arbor posts, then, since it was late, I invited him to dinner. Would you like some brownies and milk?"

She poured milk for herself, then for her daughter when Zia nodded. Placing the snack plate on the table, she murmured in annoyance, "I forgot to give the brownies I made for Jeff's family to him when he left."

"It looked as if you two were about to kiss when Sammy and I pulled into the drive," Zia accused.

"We didn't," Caileen said with forced calm. She bit into a brownie, one with walnuts.

"Your hair is mussed." Zia sat in her usual spot and selected a brownie. She wolfed it down while still managing to glare at her mother.

Caileen peered at her daughter over the rim of the milk glass as she took a drink and considered the various tactics she could take to handle the situation. While a family was a unit and one member's actions could affect the others, there was also an issue of privacy.

"So is yours," Caileen said in a casual manner.

The girl was obviously taken aback by this observation, then her face took on its mulish set. "We're not talking about me."

"No, we're not," Caileen agreed equably. "Some things are private, even in a family. I might question where you're going and how long you'll be gone out of concern for your health and safety, but that's it. I give you credit for being an adult and in control of your personal life. I expect the same from you."

"So you are involved with Jeff Aquilon," was Zia's harsh-toned conclusion.

"We're two adults with many common interests—mortgages, children, homes that need repairs." She laughed softly although it took an effort. "I think he feels sorry for me in light of my maintenance skills."

"Oh."

Caileen studied the thoughts and emotions that flitted over her child's face and saw that Zia accepted this explanation of Jeff's being at the house. It was easier than acknowledging her mother might be attractive as a woman to a man the girl was also drawn to.

Zia finished off two more brownies, downed the rest of her milk and stood. "I'm going to bed. Wake me if I don't get up in the morning. I have a test during first period, and I don't want to be late."

"I'll make sure you're up before I leave for work," Caileen promised.

When she was alone, she remained at the table, lost in thought. She knew the psychology of mothers and daughters being in competition for a husband's or father's attention at times, but it wasn't an issue she'd faced in the past.

She tried to consider the situation between her and Jeff, but her mind went into a blurry whirl of thoughts and feelings she couldn't define. She didn't want to hurt her daughter, she didn't want to be hurt, but she couldn't bring herself to regret the evening with him.

Her heart swelled as she yearned for things that seemed always beyond her reach. Her breathing became shallow and difficult. Pressing a hand to her aching chest, she sighed heavily. She didn't know what she wanted, where she was going, what the future might hold.

And what had happened to her philosophy not to take things too seriously? A hundred years from now what difference would this particular bump make in her life?

With another heartfelt sigh, she straightened the kitchen and went to bed.

"Hi. Remember me?"

Caileen started guiltily upon seeing Jeff on Wednesday when she came out of her office and squinted against the bright sunshine. She managed a calm smile. "I think so," she said, but with exaggerated uncertainty.

He'd called twice that week and left messages on her answering machine. Not sure what to say to him, she'd ignored the requests to call him.

"I got the check for the posts and material," he continued. "Thanks."

She'd mailed it Monday. "I'm sorry I forgot to give it to you last weekend."

"Well," he drawled, "we got kind of busy."

Heat flashed over her body. She willed it away before she broke into a sweat.

"How about lunch?" he asked. "Do you have time?"

"I was going to grab something quick and head for the park to study for my class tonight."

He fell into step with her. "Would you like a chicken basket? You can get vegetables with it. Krista says that's a better choice than fries."

Unable to refuse, she said, "Yes, that will be fine." She castigated herself for not being in control, then decided lunch wasn't a big deal, at least not in a *majorly* big way, except she was sort of shaky inside. Okay, it was a big deal, but she could handle it. *Shut up.* Right.

They stopped at the tiny take-out kiosk and carried their food and drinks across the street to the city park.

The closest picnic area was already taken. Women sat at the tables chatting while their children played on the wooden fort and other playground equipment.

Daffodils and tulips bloomed in orderly profusion. Grape hyacinths edged rock planters filled with nodding white flowers. Several ladies from the local gardening club were weeding the mulched beds.

Caileen selected a bench under a budding oak tree where the sun would warm their backs. "This okay?"

"Fine."

She couldn't disguise the tremor in her fingers as she opened the savory lunch.

"Don't be nervous," he murmured. "I'm not going to do anything outrageous in a public park."

Her gaze flew to his. His smile was teasing and filled with wry humor. She smiled without conscious volition.

"The morning after can be so awkward," she said, disarming the situation with honesty.

"Yeah. I was worried about seeing you, too."

"Why?"

"You can get on my case in more ways than one."

"I would never let a personal matter interfere with Tony's and Krista's welfare," she told him, and immediately regretted her tone. "I'm sorry. That sounded so self-righteous you're probably wondering where my halo is."

"Nah. It's right here." He touched her temple and made an arc around one side of her head. He laughed, a soft, unexpected chuckle that sent the heat through her again.

"Eat," he advised. "I don't want to keep you from your studies. Are you taking a class?"

"Teaching one, a class on marriage for couples with domestic problems. I hope the students don't ask about my personal experience. Five years of marriage and a divorce probably don't qualify me to give advice." She rolled her eyes at the absurdity of the idea.

They ate in silence for a few minutes before Jeff spoke again. "Krista reported that inviting the bully and her two friends to join in recess activities with her didn't work."

"What happened?"

"They told her to get lost. One of the girls threw a grasshopper on her. We had a family meeting last night and talked it over. Jeremy said he would tell them to leave Krista alone or else they would answer to him, but she vetoed his idea."

"Did you tell her she would have to speak to the teacher? Bullies can't be allowed to continue to threaten others. It's dangerous."

"She wants to try a couple of other things first. She said Anne of Green Gables wouldn't have given up so easily."

Caileen recognized the worry in his eyes and wished she hadn't suggested the books. "Real life doesn't always work the way things do in stories."

"Krista knows the boys and I are solidly behind her. She's asked for more time to work this out. Do you think that's a good idea?"

Caileen nodded as her throat constricted. She thought of wakeful nights when she'd stayed up, listening as her daughter struggled to breathe. She remembered trips to the hospital emergency room when fear was her only companion. If she'd had this man at her side, perhaps the terror wouldn't have been quite so daunting.

Ashamed of wanting more from her young husband than he'd been able to offer, she put the thought aside.

Jeff's chest lifted and fell in a relieved manner. "I have to agree with the boys—it's much easier to beat someone up than reason through a situation like this."

"Sometimes nothing works," she warned. "Perhaps you should ask that Krista be moved to another class."

"But she would still have to face the bully outside the classroom."

"True."

They finished their meal. "Enough of my problems," he told her. "You need to paint the arbor before the vines start growing over it. The hardware store is closing out some white paint that's nearing its expiration date. The paint is still good if you use it right away. Shall I pick up a gallon and come over this weekend?"

His gaze was direct but undemanding. There were no strings attached, she realized. "Zia and I can handle it. We need some family projects to give us some quality time."

He studied her for a minute, his gaze sympathetic. "How did things go Sunday night?"

"Okay. She wanted to know if we were, uh, dating."

Caileen groaned at how juvenile the word seemed and how inadequate it was in describing the episode between them.

"Are we?" he asked.

"No! I mean, of course not," she said more calmly. "I think our one-night stand should remain just that—a one-nighter. There's nothing between us."

He stood and stuffed their trash into the restaurant bag. "I think there is," he said casually. "Quite a bit when you add it up—the counseling, advice and all."

She tried not to think about the "and all" part of their relationship. It was perilous to the functioning of her heart and lungs. "No," she began and stopped.

It was rather pointless to protest an involvement since their lives were intertwined on more than one level.

"I should have had the nervous breakdown a couple of weeks ago," she muttered, "then maybe I would have been in a padded cell somewhere."

"And last weekend wouldn't have happened?" he asked, reading her thoughts with uncanny accuracy. "Too late, counselor. We'll just have to live with the memory."

He frowned as he aimed the crumpled bag at the trash bin and lobbed it in with one try. She sensed he was angry with her. Fine. She was angry with herself.

"I have to study," she said abruptly.

With a curt nod, he walked off and left her. She tried to concentrate on the marriage manual, but her mind kept drifting backward in time, to Sunday afternoon and a job well done, to Sunday night and an intimacy too powerful to forget.

Okay, it had been foolish, but she couldn't bring herself to be sorry. She knew he wasn't sorry, either. Worse, the hunger was still there between them.

She lifted a hand to her cheek, but resisted the urge to cover her face. "Help," she said, "I'm in over my head." She needed someone to step up and take charge because she had no idea what to do next.

Six couples filed into the conference room shortly before the class was to begin at seven. Caileen, finding the room was free, had opted to use it rather than the fifty-seat theater available to county departments.

Sitting around a table was cozier and encouraged a mutual exchange of ideas between the participants. At least, that was her theory. She hoped it worked.

The couples ranged in age from the nineteen-year-old mom and twenty-one-year-old father who'd nearly lost custody of their children, to a couple in their late fifties whose grown children had urged them to attend the class rather than divorce at this late stage of their marriage.

The wall clock's minute hand ticked upward. Seven o'clock. Twelve faces turned to her. Counting herself, there were thirteen of them in the room. She hoped this would be a lucky number for the group.

"Good evening. I'm Caileen Peters. Some of you know me." She glanced at the young couple and two others she'd worked with. "I'm a counselor with the Family Services Department. Mostly I work with families concerning their children. Some people think I'm an interfering witch. I would like to change that image...which is why I left my broomstick at home."

That brought a startled murmur of laughter from the participants and broke the ice. The relief was noticeable among the couples. Most of them probably thought they were there to be lectured on proper conduct.

After inviting the class to help themselves to coffee she'd made earlier, she began. "The family unit is the building block of civilization. The extended family became a clan, a tribe, a village. People became friends, neighbors, allies. Or enemies. When discord occurs in the family unit, every member is affected."

She led a discussion involving arguments and strife within the family. The couples were hesitant at first, but after a bit, they opened up, sharing experiences and laughing as they recognized similar situations.

At nine-thirty, she passed out the marriage manuals and asked each couple to fill out the worksheets on the leading causes of problems within their family unit for next week.

When the room was empty, she wiped down the table, returned the coffeemaker to her office and made sure the conference room was ready for the following business day.

Driving home, she realized she very much wanted the husbands and wives she'd met that evening to make it as couples, as if, by doing so, it would prove something she needed to know.

What? That people could change? That they could become wiser as they grew older?

God, she hoped so. It would be terrible to go through life making the same mistakes again and again.

Her thoughts went to Jeff. She'd made a foolish error in succumbing to the passion between them. Even as she admitted this fact, the flow of blood through her body seemed to speed up and hum with excitement.

She pulled under the carport behind the cottage, turned off the engine and sat there, lost in a trance-like state of swirling emotions, none of which she could identify with surety, other than the mad passion that had haunted her since meeting the intriguing veteran/artist/foster parent.

How, she wondered ruefully, could she help others with their problems when she couldn't figure out her own?

Quietly unlocking the back door and entering the house, she slipped off her shoes and padded down the hallway. Zia's door was open. Caileen paused and gazed inside.

Moonlight illuminated her daughter's form. Zia slept curled into a fetal position on her right side. Her favorite old teddy bear was propped on the other pillow, as if guarding her rest.

A surge of maternal tenderness spread through Caileen, a slow, sweet river of love and joy and happy memories. In caring for this other human creature, one who was so deeply a part of her life, she'd become a better person.

This loving, laughing delightful *other* had focused her thinking outside her own little world, a world that had been self-centered and irresponsible in a thoughtless, happy-go-lucky way. Having a child whose needs were greater than her own had helped her grow up.

The press of tears, which she hadn't experienced in several days, brought a nostalgic mood with them.

She wished she could go back to the time when she could freely cuddle her daughter in her arms.

At any rate, she vowed as she went to her room, she would never, ever do anything to cause her child harm, not even pound her on the head for falling for Sammy-the-dropout, she added with wry honesty. But she did think about it once in awhile. Smiling, she went to bed.

Jeff derided his intentions, which he chose to describe as "neighborly," while he paid for a gallon of white paint and one of green. Since he lived several miles from Caileen's cottage, he would have to extend the boundaries of his neighborhood by quite a bit.

Arriving at her place at three on Saturday afternoon, he found her on the patio, fingers flying over the keyboard of a laptop computer. She was totally unaware of him.

"Hey, there," he called out before approaching.

Startled, she looked up. "Well, hello," she said, her smile more than a bit wary.

He removed the two buckets of paint from the back of the pickup. "The sale ends today. I figured you'd forgotten to pick these up."

"I did," she admitted.

She was barefoot, a fact he noted with more than usual interest. It made her seem younger, more vulnerable.

"Monday's forecast predicts rain so it would be

a good idea to get these posts painted before then." He placed the buckets on the patio and checked the arbor as if looking for flaws they might have missed.

In truth, he was trying to keep from staring at her. She seemed to grow lovelier each time he saw her.

Her hair was held up on the top of her head with a jeweled clip. Wavy tendrils drifted around her face and down her neck, stirring with each puff of spring breeze. She wore shorts and a knit top that hugged her torso. The outline of straps over her shoulders indicated she wore a bra.

He recalled she hadn't had one on last week.

The rush of blood through his body reminded him to stick to the business at hand.

What business? some sly part of him inquired.

Painting, he responded irritably.

She closed the laptop and stood. "That was very kind of you. Let me get my purse and pay you right now. Otherwise, I'll have to send you another check."

Jeff stood in the middle of the patio while she dashed inside as if an ax murderer were after her.

He snorted in disgust. He certainly didn't have torture in mind. But there were things they could do that brought intense pleasure—

"Damn," he muttered. To distract his thoughts, he gave each support post a tug. Yep, all sound and secure.

She came outside. "How much was the paint?"

He told her.

She counted out the exact change.

His palm burned where the tips of her fingers brushed his skin as she laid the bills and coins in place.

"Thank you so much," she said.

He nodded. "No problem. I had to go by the store anyway."

They stood there in the afternoon sunlight. He tried to think of something to say.

"Would you…?" she began.

"Would you…?" he said at the same instant. He gestured toward her. "Ladies first."

"Would you care for something to drink? I have iced tea."

"That would be nice."

He followed her into the house. "If you have time, we could get the arbor painted before dark."

She flashed him an amused glance, then concentrated on filling two glasses the same distance from the rim. She handed one to him.

"And then?" she asked.

He knew a trick question when he heard one. "And then what?"

"We're not…" She took a deep breath before beginning the lecture he was expecting. "Last weekend wasn't the beginning of a grand passionate affair."

He knew it was the kind of question that invited trouble, but he asked it anyway. "Mmm, what kind of affair would you say we're starting?"

"None! We're not starting anything. I thought I made that clear…."

Her voice trailed off as exasperation played across her lovely face. He liked the way sunbeams picked out golden streaks in her light brown hair, along with a glint of silver here and there. He liked the matching gold flecks in her eyes, like hidden treasure in the sea-green depths.

"Stop that," she demanded, her knuckles going white as she clenched the iced-tea glass.

He stopped the fascinated perusal of her features. "Sorry. I like looking at you," he admitted with a candor unusual for him.

Around women, he tended to keep his thoughts to himself. Life was easier that way. Around this woman, he seemed to forget all the lessons previously learned.

Mostly, he just wanted to kiss her. And kiss her. And kiss her. Okay, and maybe a couple of other things.

She spun around and set the glass on the counter with a little bang. "You're still staring."

"Yeah, I know." He gave a snort of ironic laughter. "I'd better leave before you call the cops."

Her sigh kept him rooted to the spot. "No, stay. It's okay. I'm just a bit unnerved about being alone with you."

"Zia isn't here?"

"No. She's off on her own pursuits as usual on the weekend."

At her brief forced laughter, he wanted to take her in his arms and comfort her.

That, he realized, was where they always started

before the passion took over and concern became hot, sweet kisses.

"Things might not always be easy. Life has a way of making a person sit up and take notice," he told her, unable to clear the huskiness from his voice.

When she glanced over her shoulder, her gaze was sad and vulnerable and bruised. "It does."

"I can't stand it when you look like that," he murmured, taking the fatal step toward her.

"Like what?"

"Like you need my comforting. Like you need *me.*"

She turned to him. "I do," she said, her manner resigned, fretful, *yearning.* "I shouldn't. But I do."

He took her into his arms. Tender loving care and passion blended flawlessly, he found. Together they were a force to be reckoned with…as soon as his brain got around to thinking again.

Chapter Nine

With rollers in hand, they each took a side of the arbor and painted the new posts, then the overhead supports. They met in the middle when they finished.

Caileen experienced the usual tingle as his arm brushed against hers. When they'd kissed ninety minutes ago, she'd felt more than simple electricity. A mad rush of mixed emotions had assailed her senses. It was Jeff who'd pulled back and suggested they get to work, his voice husky but his dark eyes filled with devilish amusement at their plight.

While she wasn't surprised at the attraction, she was somewhat mystified by the laughter that had bubbled up inside her for no good reason.

Ha-ha. The joke was on her, she mused, but with a

smile. A relationship with a man who made her laugh couldn't be all bad—arggh, what was she thinking?

She arched her back in a luxurious stretch. Tilting her head, she admired their handiwork. "An excellent job," she said, satisfaction threaded through the words.

Jeff removed the used rollers from the holders and wrapped them in a plastic grocery bag. "Now you're ready for the rain predicted for Monday. By the end of summer, the roses and clematis will cover the structure again."

She indicated the rollers. "There's a hose at the side of the house. Let me wash those out while the paint is still fresh so you can reuse them."

"They were on sale, two for a dollar. I think we can afford to throw them away."

"But is that environmentally sound?"

"Yes," he said firmly, giving her a smile over his shoulder as he carried the remaining paint to the storage shed and placed the rollers in the back of his pickup.

Frowning, she went inside, washed her hands and replenished their iced-tea glasses. She'd wanted to argue with him, and his refusal to cooperate irritated her.

Honestly, her emotions had more ups and downs than a roller coaster of late. But that was to be expected with a midlife crisis, she decided, and then laughed again.

Back outside, she handed him his glass and settled in one of the patio chairs after he gallantly removed the plastic cover that had protected it from the paint and arranged the furniture in a comfortable grouping.

"Tired?" he asked, taking a seat opposite her.

"Not really."

"Good. How about going out to dinner at the Roadhouse? Their barbecued ribs are the best in town."

She opened her mouth to refuse.

"We'll make it an early night," he promised, his manner easy. "I'll come by for you at six. We'll be home by nine."

Glancing at the cottage, she was reminded of its emptiness. Zia was staying over at a friend's and wouldn't be home until Sunday afternoon. Caileen had let her daughter keep the car for the overnight outing, so she wasn't planning on going anywhere.

"Okay," she heard herself say.

He smiled and finished off the tea. She noted the movement of his throat as he swallowed, the length of his fingers as he set the glass on the table, the lines that bracketed his mouth as he smiled again.

When he rose, she did, too. She walked with him to the truck, thanked him for his help and waved while he drove off. Then she rushed into the house to shower, her mind busily running through her clothing for something stylish, yet casual.

Shortly before the hour, she surveyed the denim skirt and red knit, long-sleeved top with a critical eye. It wasn't new, but she thought it would do.

After securing the hair around her face in a

crystal clip, she slipped earrings into the three holes in her left ear and the two in her right, although she rarely wore more than a single pair anymore. Her parents had disliked her "flamboyance," as they termed it. No matter. Tonight she felt defiant, perhaps even reckless. Definitely in a "flamboyant" mood.

Outside a vehicle pulled into the drive. Heart pounding, she dashed to the kitchen in time to see Jeff cross the refurbished patio.

"I'm ready," she said, sounding a little breathless as she joined him. She hitched the strap of her purse over her shoulder and locked the door. He took her arm as he escorted her to the dark blue pickup, which was now shiny and clean.

"You washed your truck," she murmured when he opened the door and helped her up.

He looked pleased. "The kids did it. They thought the chariot, as they termed it, needed special attention for our date. I told them it wasn't a date," he added when she automatically started to protest.

"That was nice of them," she said. "I appreciate their efforts."

"Thanks."

They were silent after that.

The problem, she mused on the way to the restaurant, was that this *seemed* like a date. She felt giddy, giggly and utterly ridiculous. She didn't know what he expected….

At the restaurant, she hopped out before he could

come around the truck. Since this wasn't a date, she wasn't going to act as if it were.

The glance he gave her indicated he knew exactly what she was thinking. Oddly, his smile was sympathetic.

She was acutely aware of his hand on her back as he escorted her inside the rustic stone building. Electric tingles flowed from the spot to every nerve ending in her body. She wondered if she were glowing like a beacon in the dim light of the restaurant as they followed the hostess to their table.

"Oh, this is nice," she murmured, gazing out the window at the view after they were seated.

The restaurant perched over a ravine. A trickle of water ran along the rocky bottom. The tops of cottonwoods bent gracefully in the evening breeze. To the west, the sun was setting beyond the mountains, gilding the lower edge of a line of clouds in rosy hues of gold.

An odd sense of peace flowed into her.

After consulting her tastes, Jeff ordered a bottle of wine. "The storm is moving in earlier than the weatherman predicted," he said, his eyes studying the clouds.

She gave a hum of agreement, too lazy to shape her mouth into words. Deep inside, hovering beyond the contentment, was her own gathering storm, one of passion, made manifest by the little sizzling flashes of lightning that rumbled in the distant reaches of her mind.

"You're thoughtful," her escort observed. "Still wondering if it's wise for us to be together?"

She laughed, surprising them both. "I know it isn't. But I don't care," she added, as if defying the fate that had forbidden her to have fun.

His eyes darkened as he perused her with an intensity that brought the lightning flashes closer to the forefront of her consciousness and ruffled the air of contentment. His expression remained solemn.

The wine steward brought the merlot to the table. While Jeff tasted the wine and pronounced it "perfect," she stared at his hands, inexplicably filled with the memory of his caresses, of how tender he was, how demanding and exciting, how generous in his passion.

She wanted him with every fiber of her being.

Dear God, she was going insane. She had to stop thinking like this. Control, that was the key. She had to take charge of her emotions—

"Good evening. Are you ready to order?" the waiter asked.

Caileen glanced helplessly at the menu, then at Jeff.

"Two rib specials," he said, filling the pause. "They have a great baked sweet potato and slaw for side dishes. Would you like to try them?"

She nodded.

"Anything else to drink?" the young man asked.

"We'll stick with wine for now." When the waiter left, Jeff told her, "Mud pie is a must for dessert. This place is known for it."

"I can't figure out where you and Zia put all that you eat. I know where my extra calories go." She glanced downward to indicate her hips and thighs.

"We'll take a long walk after dinner," he promised, giving a soft laugh.

The sound filled her like the swell of violins in a rhapsody as the music rises toward the climax. Her soul also soared. A spate of longing and other emotions too deep to identify cascaded through her.

Staring at the western sky as twilight blended shades of blue and purple, she wished things could be different.

How?

She didn't know.

"Don't," he said.

Pulling back from this strange abyss of introspection, she asked, "Don't what?"

"Look sad." His attractive mouth hitched into a slight smile. "Is it because of me?"

"Not at all. I'm not sad," she assured him. "It's just that the twilight is so beautiful, it makes me feel…"

How could she describe the welter of feelings without sounding young and foolish and all the things she wouldn't, couldn't, let herself be? Oh, God, she felt like crying again.

"Fanciful?" he suggested. "My mother used to say that. 'I'm feeling fanciful today. Would anyone like to go on a picnic?' she'd ask, even though it was snowing outside."

"Did you go?"

He nodded. "In the middle of the living room. Or maybe on the porch, all bundled up and sipping hot chocolate to keep warm."

"She must have been a special person."

After a second's hesitation, he agreed. "To me, she was everything good and happy in life. Like the sun, she brought light and warmth with her."

"How wonderful to be remembered like that," Caileen said, envious of this obviously loved parent. "I don't think Zia will have kind memories of me when I'm gone."

"You may be surprised."

He refilled their wineglasses. The waiter brought each of them a bowl of slaw that had corn and red and yellow peppers in with the cabbage and carrots. A covered basket of hot rolls accompanied the slaw.

Caileen dropped the subject of children and concentrated on the food. The serenity returned. The sensual storm receded to a pleasant hum through her blood.

"This place was a good choice, just right after a busy day," she told him, taking a roll but foregoing the whipped butter. "Mmm, delicious."

"Yes," he said, but he was looking at her.

She started to reprimand him for what his eyes were saying but thought better of it. Instead, she sighed and let herself become lost in the enchantment of twilight.

After the meal, a five-piece band set up their instruments on a tiny stage. Several couples went to the hardwood square in front of the musicians.

"Shall we?" Jeff asked.

She had always loved to dance. Sometimes she waltzed around the kitchen all by herself while listening to the radio. In earlier years, Zia had taught her the newest steps, Caileen had shown her daughter the ones she knew. They'd laughed and laughed...

"Come on," Jeff murmured.

They joined the other couples as the music segued from a fast beat to a slow one. Jeff folded her into his arms, not too close, but just enough that she was aware of his body and hers, and the magnetic attraction between them. He moved very little, just a gentle shuffling back and forth.

A tremor ran over her, then another. She stepped back abruptly. "I think we should leave now."

He didn't argue. They left, and he drove her straight home. The sky was a starry canopy overhead. The bone-deep sadness returned.

"Nine o'clock, as promised," he said when he stopped in front of the empty carport.

She couldn't bear the thought of being alone. The silence would choke her. "Would you like to come in for coffee?"

"Yes."

His voice was quick and deep. It vibrated along her spine. The internal storm, like the one over the mountains, drifted closer. She hurriedly got out of the pickup and led the way across the patio.

The wind, pleasant during the day, now carried a chill down from the snow-covered peaks. She shivered as she unlocked the door and quickly entered the kitchen.

The house was comfortably warm. Thank goodness she'd set the thermostat to turn the heat on. When she dropped the keys into her purse, she missed. They fell to the floor. She scooped them up and placed them on the counter along with the purse.

Jeff followed her inside and closed the door. "I wouldn't be surprised if the storm brought snow," he told her. "It wouldn't be the first time we've had snow in April."

She put on the coffee to brew. "Two years ago we had a blizzard in May. I tried to make it to work and got stuck. Fortunately I was only a quarter mile down the road, so I walked home and spent the day here."

"I remember. The kids were still hiding out, and I was worried about them..."

His voice trailed off as the memory stirred a pool of worry and reflected concern in his eyes. She turned from this evidence of his caring nature and busied herself with cups and saucers and spoons.

If they had been together, the children wouldn't have had to run away, she thought. She and Jeff could have adopted the younger ones, and Jeremy, too, if he wanted.

Her hand jerked, causing her to drop one of the cups. It crashed to the floor and broke into shards.

"Easy," Jeff cautioned, aware of her increased nervousness the moment they arrived at the cottage. In fact, she'd been skittish all evening.

He dropped to his haunches and picked up the larger pieces of pottery while he tried to think of something to say. Assuring her of his good intentions didn't seem appropriate. He wasn't sure exactly what his intentions were at the moment.

She retrieved a broom and dustpan from a closet. "Here, let me sweep up the pieces. I don't know why I'm so clumsy tonight."

He took the items from her, swept up and tossed the slivers into the trash. "Probably the same reason I am."

She stared at him, her eyes wide but knowing.

"We do things to each other," he said with complete honesty. "It's unnerving."

After replacing the broom and dustpan on their hooks, he turned to her. Taking her hands between his, he rubbed them gently. "Your hands are cold."

"They always are when it's cold outside."

He drew her close. "You're trembling."

She looked up at him. He wondered if a person could drown from staring into someone's eyes. When she licked her lips, he almost groaned.

"I don't know what we're doing…where we're going…why this is happening…"

"I know." He kissed her on the tip of her nose and tried to smile, as if that would regain some balance between them. It didn't work. "It's damn inconvenient to feel this way."

"And scary," she added.

When she laid her head on his chest, he nearly stopped breathing. "And scary," he agreed softly, nuzzling his nose in her hair. But fear was far from his mind. She felt so right in his arms he couldn't think beyond that fact.

It came to him that, unless she told him to go, he wasn't going to be able to leave on his own. The need to hold her was too great. Okay, so he was a spineless slug where she was concerned. Worse, he didn't even care.

The coffeepot gave its final gurgle, shaking them out of the sensuous trance. He got a mug from the cabinet when she moved away. She filled both cups. Neither spoke.

They sat at the table and sipped the hot liquid while the wind murmured and the cottage creaked a bit, its joints old but sturdy as the storm became stronger.

They tried to talk, but the words kept dying on their tongues. When the coffee was gone, he knew he had to go, too. "I should leave."

"Can you stay?" she asked, flooring him with the question. "If you wanted to, could you?"

His heart started a low, fierce pounding like the resounding beat of a kettledrum. A haze filtered every half thought that entered his mind and ruthlessly drove it into misty darkness. All he could think of was *her.*

He stood, but he couldn't run. His feet were planted solidly on the shiny vinyl floor. "Yes," he said. "I can stay. I want to. If you're sure it's what you want?"

There. He wasn't using pressure to persuade her. He was being fair. "Hell," he muttered. "I don't give a damn about being fair."

Her mouth was ready for his when he kissed her. She folded into him so naturally it was as if they'd been cut in half and were now rejoined.

This time he did groan as hunger pulsed through every nerve. He rubbed up and down her back, liking the strength of her, the yielding of her flesh under his hands, the way she accepted his touch.

When she arched against him and locked her arms around his neck, he lifted her from the floor and walked into the hall. Carefully he made his way to the back of the house.

"Here?" he asked, pausing at an open door.

"No, the next one. On the left."

In her room he kicked the door closed although they were alone in the house. When he set her on her feet, she reached around him and locked the door.

"Just in case," she said.

He chuckled. "Once a parent, always a parent."

She sighed and nodded. "Always."

"But for now," he said in a half whisper, drawing her close once more, "we're a man and a woman, we're alone and I've wanted to do this all evening."

He bent to her neck and pulled the material of her top aside. He left a trail of kisses in the hollows around her throat.

"Red turns me on," he told her, "but can we take the top off now? I want to see only you."

"Yes," she said. "Yes. Yes. Yes."

He liked her answer.

They left little piles of clothing at each stop they made while crossing the braided rug to the bed. She pulled the covers down and snuggled under them while he took care of the prosthesis and then protection. He knew he wouldn't want to stop once they were in bed.

The hunger was like the last time—demanding and fiery and splendid. He touched her everywhere, then followed the caresses with his mouth, exploring her thoroughly until the taste and scent and feel of her filled all his senses.

She pleased him with her little cries of encouragement, the gasps as her passion flamed ever higher. When she went utterly still, he let her rest a moment before driving her over the edge. Her shuddering climax satisfied something primitive in him.

After a bit, she whispered, "Now it's my turn."

With soft laughter, as if she were after revenge—sweet revenge!—she paid him back in kind, stroking, nipping, licking him until he could take no more.

With controlled hunger, he turned them so she was on her back. "Take me in you," he requested, carefully holding his weight off her.

"With pleasure," she told him and did so.

Then, looking into her eyes, he began moving,

slowly at first, then faster as she guided him in the rhythm she desired. He closed his eyes as the need became unbearable. They surged together and it was bliss and peace and all the things he hadn't dared dream of in a long time.

When they at last rested, panting slightly, a sense of total possession came over him.

Mine, he wanted to shout. *This woman is mine!*

He refrained from such foolishness, but it didn't diminish the feeling. He didn't even understand it, never having felt this way before.

With a sigh, he tucked her close and pushed the confusion aside. One thing he knew—he'd never felt this degree of contentment in his life. He couldn't even open his eyes, he was so relaxed.

Caileen drifted like a strand of seaweed in a warm ocean, going where the current took her. When she realized Jeff was asleep, she eased her head from his shoulder. He turned onto his back.

Freed from his embrace, she tiptoed into the bathroom and closed the door. Closing her eyes, she let the tears come, unable to keep them inside any longer.

How could a person be happy and sad at the same time?

The problem was she wanted to be nineteen again, fresh and eager, ready to start the grand adventure of life. She wanted to be innocent and trusting. She wanted to entwine her future with the man who had just made her feel precious and beautiful and cherished.

But the road of life was one way. She could never be that young, trusting girl again. She had responsibilities. So did Jeff. Both of them had to think of Jeremy, Tony and Krista, not to mention her daughter.

She splashed water on her face and felt somewhat better. In the morning she would have a long talk with Jeff. She couldn't be involved with him and be an impartial counselor to the orphans in his care. She would have to turn the case over to another counselor.

Returning to the bedroom, she stood there for a few seconds before silently slipping between the covers.

"Where were you?" he asked sleepily. "I missed you."

He laid an arm across her waist and a thigh over her legs in a sweet intimacy that she couldn't reject. She slid her cold toes down his leg, realizing once again that she'd never even noticed the absence of his left foot. There were so many other things to be aware of at the moment.

The sadness settled over her like a veil of darkness. With the dawn she had to tell him goodbye.

Caileen woke to unusual warmth. Jeff was at her back, his body cupped around hers.

"Time to get up?" he asked, moving away from her to stretch and yawn.

"If you're ready." She thought of a possible

problem. "Uh, will your family be wondering where you are?"

"I think Jeremy will have a good idea. He told me not to worry about getting home at a decent hour."

She groaned. "What an example we're setting." Rolling to the side of the bed, she forced herself to leave the comfy nest and pull on a set of sweats. After donning thick socks, she headed for the kitchen. By the time Jeff joined her, she had coffee made and was preparing breakfast.

"Blueberry pancakes are my favorite for Sunday morning," she told him, forcing a smile. "Is that okay with you?"

"Sure." He helped himself to coffee.

Standing at the counter, he gazed outside at the thick covering of clouds. A fine mist fell, sweeping fitfully this way and that in the chilly wind. The furnace blew heat into the cottage.

"It's cold this morning," he noted, then smiled in her direction. "In more ways than one."

She nodded and took up the last pancake. After putting the plates on the table, she said, "It's ready."

They talked in brief sentences during the meal, mostly about the weather. Finally he suggested, "Why don't you say what's on your mind?"

His manner was patient but wary. She gazed into his eyes, both of their faces serious. "I have to turn your case over to someone else. Even if we refrain from…from further involvement, our relationship has gone beyond what's acceptable. This has never happened to me before," she added and winced at how miserable and guilty she sounded.

A sigh escaped her. She *was* miserable and guilty.

"I realize that. Do you have someone you trust to hand our case over to?"

"I'll check with my supervisor."

"And then?" he asked.

She didn't pretend to misunderstand. "I don't think it would be wise for us to see each other. We're too volatile when we're together."

"Mmm," he said.

She wasn't sure if she was pleased or not that he seemed to be taking her decision so calmly.

"So," she said with finality. "I'm glad we're in agreement on this."

He pushed his empty plate aside and looked her in the eye. "But we're not. If you're not on our case, what's to keep us from seeing each other?" He paused and smiled in a slow, sexy way. "From dating?"

Tension gathered in her neck and shoulders. "The children. Surely you can see it's impossible."

He shook his head.

"You're as stubborn as my first husband was," she snapped and was immediately appalled. Past relationships were not a good thing to bring up in an argument.

"You're not so bad in that department yourself," he mocked softly.

She tried to read his mood, but his expression was opaque. She suddenly felt shut out and alone, as if she had to pit her uncertain strength against the world the way she had years ago.

"I'm not having, starting, continuing—whatever!—an affair with you," she stated, making her position perfectly clear in resounding bell tones.

The kitchen door opened. Zia stood on the threshold as if turned to stone. She looked from Caileen to Jeff and back to Caileen. "This is…this is too disgusting," she said and slammed the door so hard the glass rattled in it and the window over the sink.

"Zia, wait!"

Caileen rushed to the door, but her daughter was already backing out into the road. With rubber whining and gravel spewing, the family sedan skittered side to side, then shot down the country lane in a fury. When the car disappeared from sight, only the morning chirp of birds broke the silence.

A hand settled on her shoulder. "She'll be okay," Jeff said. "She'll settle down in a bit."

"What if she doesn't?"

"We'll call her boyfriend and see if she's with him."

"Yes," Caileen agreed. "Yes, that's where she'll go."

She returned to the table and sank into a chair. "I think you should leave. Last night was a terrible mistake."

It hurt to say the words, she found, even though it was true. She'd been selfish and careless to let desire overtake her better judgment. It just wasn't in the cards for her to have a great love….

"Only if we let it be," he told her, his gaze unwavering. "Kids have to learn that parents have lives, too."

Anger and guilt tore at her. "When did you get to be so wise? You don't even have kids of your own." She pressed a hand over her mouth. "I'm sorry. That was hateful."

A muscle moved in his jaw. He went to the door. "I'll call later today to make sure Zia is okay." He hesitated. "We'll talk about us another time. When things settle down." He left, closing the door gently behind him.

Caileen sat there and forced air into her lungs, one breath, another…another… When she felt calm enough, she dialed Sammy's number.

"She isn't here," he said. "I don't expect she will be. We broke up last night."

Shocked, Caileen hung up and clung to the counter. No wonder Zia had been upset and had come home earlier than expected. Her heart was breaking.

While she and Jeff had been indulging their senses, her child's life had been falling apart. Where would the girl go when her home was no longer a sanctuary?

Caileen had no answer. She paced the floor for most of the day after calling Zia's best friends and learning she hadn't turned up at any of their houses. As the sun went down, she stared at the phone and wished she had someone to comfort her.

Only one name came to mind, and that was the one she couldn't call on. She couldn't indulge her own needs and weaknesses while her daughter was missing.

Chapter Ten

Because Zia was "of age," Caileen knew what many parents learned the hard way—an adult who left home wasn't considered a runaway or a missing person by the local authorities. As a counselor, she was aware of this, but emotionally she found it difficult to accept when she checked with the authorities in case her wayward child had had an accident.

Upon hearing she and her daughter had had a "sort of disagreement," the police detective lost all interest. "She'll come home when she's ready," he'd said.

Caileen worried, wrung her hands and paced the floor all day Sunday. As night descended, the telephone rang.

She jumped for it and answered in a choked voice, "Hello? Zia? Hello?"

"It's Jeff."

Caileen slumped into the sofa. "There's been no word from her."

"The boyfriend didn't hear from her, either?"

"They broke up last night."

Jeff muttered an expletive. "She's having a rough time." He hesitated, then asked, "Have you spoken with her father yet?"

"With Brendon? No." It had been so long since she'd thought of her ex as a helpmate in raising their daughter that the idea was totally foreign to her.

"She might have gone to him. Where's he located?"

"He's building a subdivision of condos in a golfing community in northern Oregon. He lives in Portland now."

"I see."

Caileen thought she detected a note of reprimand in the words. A tempest of anger bubbled in her. She quickly suppressed it. She had enough on her plate without giving in to petty emotions.

"You're right," she murmured. "Perhaps she did go to her father. I suppose that's logical."

"Well, I don't really know," he said, conceding that he might not be the all-wise one on family dynamics. "But it seems worth trying."

"I'll call him. And Jeff? Thanks for the suggestion."

"Sure."

The hum of the phone line made her aware of

time passing and that she should hang up. She didn't want to break the connection to him, though. She wished he were here with her, consoling her with his quiet presence.

No, no. She didn't need anyone.

"One other thing," he finally said. "How do you plan on getting to work?"

"I haven't thought that far ahead." She considered. "One of the other counselors lives within a mile of my place. I can get a ride in with her tomorrow."

"And then?"

She rubbed her forehead. It was too hard to think. "I can walk. Exercise is good."

"Pete at the garage on Main Street has loaners for his customers. I called him at home. He says you can use one of those for a few days."

Tears burned behind her eyelids at this kindness from strangers. "That's nice of him. Thanks for your help on this. I didn't think about being stranded."

His soft chuckle was soothing. "That's what friends are for. If you need anything, let me know. Okay?"

"Yes. Well, I'll call you later. If I hear anything," she added, projecting a firmness she was far from feeling, as if all was sure to work out just fine.

Yeah, right.

For a second, she felt as if her entire life had been a charade, with her pretending to be resolute and in control of every situation while inside she quavered in fear and doubt with feelings of inadequacy.

"Good night," he said.

"Good night."

She held in the button when he hung up, then waited for the dial tone. From her own little black book, she located Brendon's number and called his cell phone. The line hissed and crackled when he answered.

She had to clear her throat before she could speak. "Brendon? It's Caileen."

"Yeah. I was expecting your call."

"You were?" Relief washed through her. "Then Zia *is* at your place. When did she get there?"

"Uh, a couple of hours ago."

She started to ask why he hadn't called to let her know, then thought better of it. "What did she tell you?"

He gave a bark of laughter. "That she was moving in. Don't worry," he quickly added, "I set her straight on that score right away."

"As in?" she asked, gloom settling on her shoulders like Poe's raven.

"As in, she was welcome to visit for a while, but with only one bedroom—I use the other for my office—my apartment wasn't suitable for more than one."

Caileen's heart sank. "Did she storm out?"

"Yeah." He sighed. "Kids."

Caileen could hear the shrug in his voice and had to suppress anger at what seemed to her his refusal to accept any responsibility for their daughter's welfare.

"So you don't know where she is now?" she asked.

"Probably on her way back to Idaho. I told her to get over her snit, go home and finish her schooling."

This was certainly a departure from what he'd told *her* twenty-one years ago when he'd laughed at her hesitation to quit school and drive off into the sunset with him.

A headache pounded with sudden ferocity behind her right eye. Caileen rubbed the spot and tried to think. "She broke up with her boyfriend—"

"And found you having Sunday morning breakfast with a man who had apparently spent the night at your place," her former husband interrupted, amusement in his tone. "I told her to grow up."

Tears filled Caileen's eyes, closed her throat. Of all the times for Brendon to act the stern disciplinarian, this was possibly the worst. She wondered if life could possibly get any more disappointing for the nineteen-year-old.

If only *she'd* acted like a responsible parent instead of a sex-starved divorcée….

"Hey, you okay?" he asked.

Other than feeling she would break into fragments at a glance, she was fine. She bit back the sarcastic remark.

"I'm worried," she said instead.

"Ah, you know kids. They dramatize a hangnail. She'll come around. After all, she has a level head on her shoulders. Just like her mom," he added with only a trace of sardonic amusement.

"Yeah, right," she managed to reply in the same tone. "Call me if you hear from her. I'll do the same."

"Right."

After replacing the receiver, Caileen couldn't help but recall that in her years of working with Family Services she knew of three teenagers who had committed suicide. None of them had been one of her cases, but still, it made one stop and think.

"No," she said to the empty room. "Zia wouldn't…she wouldn't…"

She went back to pacing and watching the clock. At midnight, she pulled a fleece blanket around her and slept on the sofa. She woke shortly after one and listened to the sound of a vehicle on the road. It passed by the house without slowing down.

Gazing out the window, she noted that clouds covered the sky. No moon. No friendly star to light the way home. It was one of the darkest nights she'd ever known.

Rain fell in a steady, disconsolate drizzle on Monday morning. It continued off and on for the rest of the week.

On Wednesday, Caileen faced the marriage class feeling like the world's biggest fraud. She guided the discussion through each item of discord on the couples' lists and had them consult the marriage manual on ways to defuse tense situations. In the second half of the session, she had them practice listening to their partners' complaints, then each person had to write down what they'd heard and present an idea of how to handle the problem in their own marriages.

All in all, it was a productive meeting.

At ten, she arrived home in a heavy mist. The bleakness of the cottage assailed her. Once she'd thought of it as her personal haven, an anchor in life's storms for her and her asthmatic child. Now it merely felt empty.

Thursday was the day she'd set aside for family visits that week. She planned to drop in unannounced at six homes. Three of them were biological families and three were foster families. The first three were neat and peaceful.

She brought puppets and played games with the younger children, listening carefully to their chatter and observing how they treated the puppet family.

During lunch and an afternoon break, she wrote up her notes, then headed for the next place. It was after six when she stopped at the home of the young couple who'd nearly lost their children in a custody battle with the paternal grandparents.

She could hear the parents quarreling when she got out of the car. Through the front windows, she saw the baby was in a swing, crying while it tried to suck its fingers. The two-year-old was jumping on the sofa. The television was on, but no one was paying any attention to it.

The husband stood on the living room side of the breakfast bar while the wife was on the kitchen side.

Each was trying to get his or her point across. Neither listened to the other's view.

Caileen knocked loudly.

A hush fell over the occupants of the house while the television continued to blare the latest news of world atrocities. The husband came to the door.

"Hi," she said with a solemn smile. "It looks as if I've arrived at the right time. May I come in?"

He shrugged and stood aside.

The mother rushed around the counter and picked up the baby, shushing it and welcoming her at the same time. "Get off the sofa," she ordered the other child.

After straightening the cushions, she invited Caileen to have a seat. Her husband turned off the television.

"That's better," Caileen said. "Noise adds to the tension when things aren't going right, doesn't it?"

Using techniques from the marriage manual, she tried to gently lead the couple in exploring mutual ways to help each other with the stress in their daily lives. The father suggested that he take the kids off his wife's hands while she prepared the evening meal. They decided to take turns bathing the children and cleaning up the kitchen. While she nursed the baby, he would read to the older child and settle her into bed.

On weekends, he would have Saturday morning free and she would have the afternoon. Sunday afternoons would be devoted to family fun such as trips to the park or visiting their families or having friends over.

Caileen wrote the agreement down while the mom and dad put the youngsters to bed. The couple signed the form as a contract, with both agreeing to review the provisions at a monthly family meeting.

Satisfied that they'd made a breakthrough in their dealings with each other, Caileen bid them good night and left the now peaceful abode.

It was after ten when she got home. As usual, it was dark and unoccupied. The message light was blinking on the phone when she entered the kitchen. She rushed to the instrument and hit the Replay button.

"Uh, this is Jeff. I just wanted to check in with you. Jeremy reported that Zia wasn't in history class today. I suppose you haven't heard from her?"

"Hey, Brendon here. I'm leaving for a weekend at the coast. Call me on the cell phone if Zia shows up. I'm getting a little worried at not hearing from either of you."

In the background, Caileen heard a woman's voice and realized her former husband was probably going off on a long weekend with his current girlfriend.

A hot tide of fury roiled through her. She wanted to scream and curse and throw things, to cast aside civilized behavior in favor of venting the primitive rage that tore at her insides. Most of all, she wanted to find her daughter.

Pressing a hand to her forehead, she hit the delete

button on the answering machine. She wasn't up to talking to anyone tonight. After eating a sandwich and a bowl of canned soup, she showered and went to bed shortly after eleven.

The wind howled down from the mountain and the rain changed from mist to icy droplets. It beat against the windows in a chilling staccato.

Going into Zia's room, Caileen picked up the teddy bear and returned to bed, finally going to sleep with the cuddly toy tucked under her chin.

Jeff stood at the open door of the shop and watched the rain come down in a steady drizzle. At least the wind had quit gusting with gale force sometime after midnight.

A few tree limbs had blown down, he noted, but mostly the land was covered in shades of spring green, looking fresh and promising after the long winter.

He wondered if the missing girl had shown up yet, but refrained from calling. Caileen had said she would call if she heard anything.

Returning to the sculpture, one that was commissioned for the second home of a Chicago businessman, he flexed a copper band, crimped it into the desired shape and soldered it into place, then stood back to check the effect. This female figure was quite different from the pioneer woman he'd delivered to the bank plaza a few days ago.

From the side, the copper band formed the perfect

curve of a woman's breast—full and erotic, the nipple beaded, suggesting passion. He traced the line with a forefinger.

It was *her* form, he realized.

His breath quickened. His body reacted with a hard surge of hunger and longing that was painful.

He wasn't surprised. The lovely counselor had filled his dreams all that week. He'd awakened to emptiness and had faced each day with a restlessness that was new to him. The net result was an irritability that he'd tried to conceal from the kids.

Krista's problems with the bully were ongoing. At the weekly family meeting, she had finally agreed to go with him to the principal come Monday morning. If things didn't change, he was considering home schooling, no matter that he didn't know a damn thing about it.

Directing his mind to the project at hand, he studied the sketches he'd made for the sculpture. He and the client had faxed drawings back and forth until they'd come up with a representation of the basic idea.

The businessman had wanted a female form, one that represented strength and grace, a nurturing presence for the mountain retreat, which would be a log home of more than 5000 square feet when finished.

Jeff smiled wryly at the size of the place. The "rustic" lodge was twice the size of his house and had more amenities than an island resort.

Except for a beach. He envisioned walking through white sand along a faraway shore, the sun warm on his back, a beautiful woman at his side, her eyes the exotic green of the sea....

With a curse, he tossed the sketch on the worktable and returned to the statue. Over a copper sheeting form that suggested the structure of the body, he was adding layers to indicate the delicate curves of the female.

The strength of the bones. The beauty of the flesh. That's what he wanted to depict.

He began shaping the curve of a hip, stopping often to hold the piece up to the figure. Finally he thought he had it right. He worked through lunch and into the afternoon with three interruptions from builders who needed various moldings and appliances for their clients.

Jeremy brought the younger kids home from school. They changed clothes and joined him in the shop.

"Looks great," his nephew said, walking all around the form. "Is she anyone we know?"

Jeff felt heat flow up his neck and lodge in his ears. He groaned silently. "She's the answer to my prayers. Too bad I can't make her come alive."

Jeremy studied him, then the statue. "It may happen," he said cryptically and winked at the other two.

Jeff ignored the remark. "How did it go today?" he asked Krista.

"I got a hundred on the spelling test."

"Way to go," he complimented. He waited.

The eleven-year-old took a deep breath before adding, "I refused to leave when Sidney told me to get lost during recess. When she threatened to hit me, I said that would be a mean thing to do. I told her we could all play and have fun or we could go to the teacher."

"Were you scared?" Tony asked.

"Not too scared," Krista told him. "I've been practicing what to say all week like Uncle Jeff said."

Jeff held out his hand to the brave little girl. She threw her arms around his waist and pressed her face against him. "That took a lot of courage," he murmured, stroking her thick hair. "What did she do?"

"Nothing, but her friends threw sand on me. I said I wasn't leaving, no matter what they did.

"Sidney said no one wanted me, that's why I had to live in a foster home." The child gazed at him, her expression earnest and sure. "I told her that you and Jeremy wanted me and my brother and that you'd told the judge so in court. That shut her up."

Jeff nodded and asked in reasonably calm tones, "Did you go to the teacher, sweetheart?"

"Not right then. My friend Roberta told Sidney and her friends that no one was ever going to play with them again if they didn't start being nice to everybody. They threw sand on her, too. After recess, she went with me to the teacher. Sidney and the other two were called to the principal's office just before the sixth period bell rang."

"We'll have to see how it goes from here," Jeff said. "If there's any more trouble, I'll talk to the principal. No one has the right to threaten or hurt other people." He scooped Krista up and placed her on his shoulder. "Let's head for the house. Let's see, it's Tony's turn to cook dinner, isn't it?"

"What are we having?" Jeremy asked. "I really liked that green stuff with the pineapple and carrots."

Krista giggled because in truth Jeremy had acted as if he were being poisoned when he'd eaten the gelatin dish.

"I got a new recipe out of a magazine," Tony said. "It's called broccoli slaw."

Jeremy clutched his chest in mock despair. "Broccoli! Yikes, he really is trying to kill us."

On this humorous note, they entered the house. The phone rang at that moment. Jeremy, being the closest, picked up the receiver. "Hello?"

He waited, then spoke the greeting again before hanging up. He shrugged. "Wrong number, I guess."

A strong instinct pinged through Jeff. He took the phone and punched in the call-back code. Caileen answered on the first ring.

"Hey, it's Jeff. Uh, did you just call?"

The beat of silence told him she considered denying it, but she answered in the affirmative. "I wondered if Jeremy had heard anything about Zia in any of his classes today. Kids usually know when couples break up and…and other things about each other."

"Have you heard anything about Zia at school?" he asked his nephew.

Jeremy gave him a quizzical glance and shook his head.

"No, sorry," Jeff said into the phone. "We'll call if we do."

"Okay. Thanks. Sorry to bother you."

He heard the worry in her voice. Her thoughts seemed disconnected, as if she were having a hard time stringing words together.

"It's no bother."

"Invite her to dinner," Jeremy told him. He looked at Tony. "If we have enough for one more?"

Tony nodded. "Sure. We're having hamburgers with the slaw. And baked beans. There'll be plenty."

"Would you like to come over and have dinner with us?" Jeff asked into the phone.

"That's very nice of you to invite me, but I think I should stay at home. Just in case."

"Another time then."

"I returned Pete's loaner car today and rode home with one of the other counselors," she said just as he started to say goodbye. "I'm thinking of looking at used cars in the morning." She paused. "Do you have an opinion on which is the best to buy?"

"There are several reliable models. I would look here first, then compare prices to those in Boise." He remembered she didn't have transportation. "I could pick you up, say around nine tomorrow?"

"Oh, I can't take up your time like that."

"Hey, what are friends for if you can't count on them in an emergency?" He kept his tone light, philosophical, but his pulse speeded up. "Besides, guys like looking at cars and kicking tires, makes us feel macho and all that."

She laughed with him, a strained sound mixed with relief. "If you're sure you don't mind, I would be eternally grateful. I seem to be overwhelmed this week."

"I know the feeling," he said, figuring she'd spent the week in various stages of frantic concern and parental guilt over her daughter. "I'll see you in the morning."

As soon as he hung up, Jeremy turned to him. "Why don't you go over tonight?" he suggested. "The kids and I will be fine here, and she could probably use some company. I won't charge you too much for babysitting these two brats."

"I don't need a babysitter," Tony protested.

"Are you going to stay all night?" Krista asked.

Jeff shook his head. "I'm staying right here with *my* family this evening. I don't want to miss that broccoli slaw."

Jeremy made choking sounds and clutched his throat. "If we live through dinner, I thought we might go to a movie tonight. I'll take you two...if Uncle Jeff pays."

"I'm going, too," Jeff volunteered.

Tony gave his older relatives a disgusted glance. "You guys want to go to the movie so you can fill up on popcorn after dinner."

"I *like* broccoli slaw," Krista said in a show of loyalty to her brother. Then she put a hand over her mouth and giggled, which made Jeff and Jeremy laugh while Tony rolled his eyes.

Later, sitting through a comedy in which the child stars saved the day for their town, Jeff's thoughts drifted far from the fictional community in the movie.

He knew Caileen blamed herself for her daughter's flight from grim reality, as he termed it to himself. Zia had been the center of her mother's world for years. To find out she might be shifted to one side was alarming, especially when she'd just broken up with her boyfriend.

While he was worried about the girl, he found he was more concerned about the mother. No one could shut off all other aspects of life and live for another, not even the brilliant counselor. Even if he weren't an expert on family dynamics, he knew that much. While he was deeply committed to the welfare of the three young people in his care, he knew an adult sometimes needed more.

And what, he questioned, was his interest in all of this?

A hot surge of blood told him his motives weren't exactly as pure as fresh snow on a mountain. He'd spent the past five years putting his life back together and getting his business up and running. There'd been little time for personal things.

But now?

He forced his attention to the movie and tried not to think about holding a sweet, warm woman in his arms…and making love with her…or sharing a meal…working on the arbor…talking…laughing…making love…

Oh, yeah, he'd mentioned that already.

Chapter Eleven

As she had all week, Caileen had trouble getting to sleep Friday night. She was therefore startled out of a sound sleep Saturday morning by a loud knocking.

A glance at the clock assured her she had overslept. She muttered an expletive, grabbed an oversized velour shirt for a robe and rushed to the kitchen. She recognized Jeff's familiar shape on the other side of the door and opened it for him.

"I'm so sorry," she said. "I overslept."

His smile was relaxed. "You and Zia must have stayed up late talking. Perhaps I should come back another time."

"No," she said, puzzled by the remark. A light dawned. "Zia! You saw her? Where? In town?"

Now he looked confused as he shook his head. "Your car is in the carport. I assumed she'd come home."

"My car?" She brushed past him and stared at the family sedan safely parked in its usual spot. Whirling, she rushed down the hall to Zia's room.

The teddy bear, which she'd replaced on the pillow after that one night of fear and loneliness, gazed forlornly at her from the unused bed.

Caileen glanced wildly around as if expecting her daughter to materialize the way people did in science fiction films. "Zia?"

"She isn't here," Jeff said, looking over her shoulder and also checking the room. "She must have left the car during the night."

"How could she do that?" Caileen demanded. "She would never walk to town in the dark."

"A friend probably followed and drove her in. Maybe she left a note in the car. I'll go see."

When he left, Caileen trailed after him down the hall and became aware of her icy feet on the cold floor. She put on a pot of coffee, went to her room to dress, then returned to the kitchen. She knew—somehow she knew—there was no note.

"Nothing in the car," Jeff said upon entering and shutting the door quietly behind him.

Caileen poured them each a cup of coffee. "She's too stubborn, too proud to come crawling home. I was the same at her age." She sighed and sat at the table, her mind dark with worry and anger and all the other useless emotions that overwhelmed her.

"And still are," he said, his tone light but his eyes sympathetic.

His hands enclosed hers, surrounding her cold fingers with warmth and strength. She knew she could lean on him if she needed to.

She pulled away. "Don't."

He was silent for a minute. "Guilt isn't going to change anything," he finally said.

"I agree, but it's still gnawing away at my conscience. If we...if I hadn't acted so stupid, this never would have happened."

"Stupid," he repeated and laughed without mirth. "I guess that lets me know what you think of our time together."

"It was a mistake. My daughter was hurt. She came home, needing refuge. Instead, she found... she found..."

"Me and you," he finished for her, giving her a level perusal that hinted at controlled anger.

Resting her elbows on the table, she covered her eyes with her hands. A headache pinged over her right eye and little darts of light flashed behind her eyelid. A migraine. Just what she needed.

"What a terrible example I've set," she muttered.

"How?" he demanded. "By providing a safe and secure place for your daughter to grow up? By working until you were ready to drop so your child would have the medical attention she needed? How often does Zia have an asthma attack nowadays?"

She removed her hands and lifted her head. "She's outgrown the illness. That sometimes happens."

"Fine. So you were guilty of being an individual and having needs of your own," he added, his voice dropping to a husky level.

"Zia needed me—"

"You were here," he cut in. "I would have left so she could pour out her heartbreak to you, but she chose to run away like a hurt child."

"She was a hurt child," Caileen whispered fiercely. Anything louder made her head pound unbearably.

"Maybe it's time she grew up."

Caileen leaped from the chair. "What do you know about it? You've never had a child of your own! I didn't want to be like my parents—so strict and unforgiving, as if they'd never been young and filled with life. I wanted her to feel secure, to explore the possibilities of her future, not fall for some dropout!"

She stood there panting, each beat of her heart reflected in the pulsating stream of color behind her right eye. The pain there intensified.

"The way you did." He stood, too. "Isn't it time you forgave yourself for that mistake? Or aren't you allowed to be human like the rest of us?"

She was silent as he walked out the door. His limp was slightly more visible as he crossed the arbor and the stone path to the driveway. She listened until the sound of his engine faded away in the far distance.

"I don't want her to be left alone with a sick child the way I was. I don't want her to be afraid...the way I was," she murmured, her voice thick with tears.

After swallowing a couple of aspirin to offset the pounding in her head, she sat at the table and drank coffee until it felt like lead in her stomach. It was almost ten before she could force herself to eat some toast and an egg.

Later she went out to the car and found it had been washed inside and out. The interior was as neat as that of a used car still on the dealer's lot.

As if her daughter had never driven away in a fury of hurt and disappointment. As if nineteen years had been but a mirage. As if her efforts to be a good parent had all been for nothing.

Returning to the house, she took another of the migraine tablets and slept fitfully on the sofa for another hour. By noon she felt as she had last weekend, too weary to move as she waited for word of her child. She called Brendon and reported that there was still no news on their daughter, but the car had mysteriously appeared.

"So she wised up and came home," he said.

"She brought the car back. She didn't stick around."

"When she runs out of money, she'll show up."

Right. Like they did when Zia was sick and they were broke and she would rather have starved than call her parents and ask for help. Zia was cut from the same cloth.

Rubbing her right eye, where the pain of the migraine reminded her of its presence with a faint but steady ping, she stifled the sarcastic remarks. "I'll call if I hear anything."

"Hey, surfer girl, you should come down and visit. We could head south and hit all the beaches. Remember the summer we did that?"

"Yes, I remember."

"The sun and the sea and riding the inside curl of a wave that went on forever." He sighed. "Those were the days."

"They were," she agreed. "Doesn't your current girlfriend surf? I thought that was the acid test women had to pass before you would ask them out."

"Ha-ha," he said. "Actually, she decided not to go. She thought a simple weekend at the coast sounded dull. As I get older, I find I like things such as quiet evenings, reading a good book or just listening to music—the things you used to want to do."

She couldn't help it. She laughed. "Are you still feeling the effects of being over forty, Brendon?"

"Maybe," he admitted, "but it isn't as bad as I'd thought it would be when I was twenty. For one thing, I'm no longer broke. Mortgage rates are low and business is good."

"That's great. Well, we should get off the phone in case our wayward daughter tries to call."

After they said goodbye, she sat there, not exactly

lost in memories, but viewing the past as if she were at a movie. She could see herself and her handsome young husband acting their parts with assurance, each believing their make-believe world would go on forever.

Then real—as opposed to reel—life had intruded and the cameras stopped rolling. The arrival of a baby had changed her world, but not Brendon's.

The migraine returned with sudden ferocity. She lay on the sofa with an ice pack over her eyes and tried to figure out where Zia might be.

Both sets of grandparents had sent their only grandchild generous checks for birthdays and Christmas over the years. The money had gone into a savings account. Her daughter had enough funds to live on for several weeks, maybe months.

That fact only increased the sense of despair and failure on her part. She'd wanted Zia to have a good start in life. With an education and money in the bank for security, the girl could follow her heart—

Caileen's thoughts came to an abrupt halt. She'd followed her heart and look where it had gotten her.

But she'd made it, she reflected after a bit. In fact, her life had been peaceful, maybe even dull, for the past few years. Hope dawned in her like a shy sun coming up after a night of terrible storms. She'd survived. So would Zia.

Pushing herself upright, she reached for the

phone and dialed a number. She owed Jeff in more ways than one.

Besides, she wanted to see him. And she wasn't going to analyze the feeling to death.

When his answering machine came on, she cleared her throat, then apologized for her earlier anger.

"If you, uh, aren't busy, I wondered if you would like to come over for dinner tonight around seven?" She waited a second. "Have a pleasant afternoon," she finished and hung up, feeling foolish.

With the headache fading, she went outside, mowed the lawn and worked in the flower beds. Tranquility flowed over her as she admired the spring blossoms close at hand, then gazed at the distant landscape.

The mountains were lovely with their caps of snow that glistened in the sunlight. The light green of oak and aspen leaf buds contrasted nicely against the dark green of the pine and fir trees.

While working she came to a conclusion—she could only change those things that she controlled. She could not dictate what others should do, and she wasn't a failure because all didn't go as planned.

She must also give her daughter the space she needed to grow up. Even as she smiled at this wise advice, a certain sadness pierced her heart.

She said farewell to the cautious, protective mother she'd been for nineteen years. It was time to write a new chapter in her own life.

Back in the house, she found a message from Jeff

accepting her invitation. Glancing at her watch, she gave an exclamation and rushed into the shower while planning the menu for the evening.

Shrimp and pasta was a quick and easy dish. Salad. Cherry cobbler for dessert.

She paused to consider her lighter mood. One, she knew her daughter was somewhere close, probably at a girlfriend's home. Two, a handsome man was coming to dinner.

Those were enough to lift any woman's spirits. From now on, she was going to appreciate the little things!

Jeff, outside in the front flower bed that ran along the stepping stone walkway, paused when he heard the ring of the phone. For a second he feared Caileen was going to cancel the dinner. He heard Jeremy answer the portable phone.

"Just a minute," Jeff heard his nephew say before leaving the living room and disappearing down the hall. A second later, he heard a door close.

A ripple of unease slithered along Jeff's neck. He had a premonition of impending disaster, although he couldn't say why. He tossed the pulled weeds into the compost pile, went inside and washed his hands at the kitchen sink.

When Jeremy returned to the kitchen, his manner was withdrawn, maybe troubled. He placed the phone on its cradle and stood there for a second.

"Problems?" Jeff asked.

The young man hesitated before saying, "Not really. Well, maybe. I need to go out for a while. I'll be back before bedtime." He glanced at Tony and Krista as if to assure them he wouldn't leave them alone for the evening.

Jeff experienced a squeezing sensation in his chest. His nephew was too young for the responsibility he'd taken on. He'd lost his youth because of it. Jeff worried that the boy didn't date, rarely went to ball games and seemed intent only on studying and getting through college as fast as possible. All work and no play…

"I, uh, might bring someone over to spend the night," Jeremy finished, looking uncertain.

Jeff realized the younger man was asking his permission to bring someone home with him. He nodded. "You know our place is always open to your friends."

"Thanks."

After Jeremy left, the younger kids, who were playing a video game, looked at him as if waiting for their cue of what to do next.

"So what do you guys want for supper?" he asked.

"We already have the menu planned," Krista reminded him, which also reminded him that she didn't like sudden changes.

What a childhood his three charges had lived through. By contrast, he thought Zia had had a life of ease.

But that was none of his business.

After he and Krista put stuffed pork chops in the oven, he took a quick shower and dressed to go over to Caileen's house. At six-thirty, he saw the younger two seated at the table with the meat, leftover broccoli slaw and applesauce.

They were discussing the possible outcomes of Krista's confrontation with the troublesome threesome, as they'd dubbed the bullies.

"Maybe now they'll be nice and want to play like everyone else," Krista suggested.

Jeff gazed at the youngster and wondered how, after her short but difficult life, she could still be so hopeful about human nature. He was worried the girls might retaliate for their imagined wrongs and really hurt Krista.

He and Jeremy would keep an eye out for the girl. And Tony would, too. The boy was protective of his sister, as a brother should be.

On the drive to her home, he wondered how Caileen was holding up. A dozen times that week he'd nearly driven over to her house to see for himself. However, since his presence last Sunday had been the final straw of contention between mother and daughter, he'd refrained from going over without an invitation.

Okay, so he'd jumped on the idea of helping her pick out a used car, but she hadn't said no.

Then they'd quarreled again. He was astute enough to know the harsh words were caused by guilt. Caileen felt her actions had pushed her daughter into running away. Jeff thought the girl could use a dose or two of reality and learn the world didn't revolve around her and her problems.

Not your business.

Remember that, he warned the part of him that wanted Caileen's attention centered on them and all the things they could do together.

The sky was awash with the colors of sunset when Jeff parked his pickup behind Caileen's car. He tried not to notice the tightening of his insides or the faster beat of his heart as he got out and walked up the path to the back door, which was open to the balmy evening air.

"Come in," Caileen called.

He went inside, but she wasn't in the kitchen. The delicious aroma of food filled the small space. The table was set for two. Soft music filled the air from the stereo in the living room.

"Hi," said a sweet, feminine voice he'd heard more than once in his dreams of late.

His hostess bustled in, still fitting an earring in her right earlobe. He thought of removing it and gently nibbling on the delectable flesh. Her black slacks and knit top added a sophisticated sleekness to her figure. With the outfit, she wore a simple gold chain around her neck.

He cleared his throat. "Something smells good."

"Cherry cobbler. It's time for it to come out of the oven. I hope you like shrimp with pasta. It's a family favorite that I haven't made in ages."

A whiff of her perfume teased his senses as she passed him on her way to the oven. She tossed him a smile, a sort of wry, offhand one that held an apology, the way her voice had when she'd left the message on the phone.

So the dinner was to make up for their disagreement?

Okay, he could handle that. He would eat, they would have a pleasant conversation—far removed from children and parental problems—he would say good night and that would be that. They would go on their merry but separate ways, except for her checking on Tony and Krista.

He didn't expect any trouble there. He was going to be the best foster father the Family Services department had ever seen.

"Are you hungry?" she asked, removing the dessert from the oven. "I'm starved. I worked in the yard this afternoon and lost track of time."

His mouth watered. "To be honest, I hadn't thought about food until I walked in here. Now I can hardly wait to sit down. Anything I can do to help?"

"There's wine in the refrigerator. If you'll open it, we should be ready to eat."

He tried not to read more into the evening than she intended, but what was that? He huffed out an exasperated breath while he popped the cork on a bottle of pinot gris.

She placed two wine goblets on the counter. He filled them to the halfway mark and carried them to the table while she brought over a basket of rolls wrapped in a napkin. Salads were already in place.

"Okay, that's it, I think," she said, scrutinizing the items on the table.

He stepped behind her and pulled out the chair.

"Thank you," she murmured.

Suppressing the urge to lean down and kiss the spot right under her ear, he quickly went to his own seat. Holding up the wineglass, he said, "Cheers."

She returned his smile. "Cheers."

During the meal, they spoke of the weather, the profusion of flowers that were in bloom, what the summer might bring.

"I'll be glad when school is out," he admitted. "Krista reported the bullies to the teacher on Friday. I'm not sure how things will go during the remaining six weeks. Jeremy or I will pick her up each day after class so she won't be alone waiting for the bus."

"Did the other girls get expelled?"

"We don't know yet." He told Caileen all that had transpired as far as he knew. She was sympathetic and interested in the outcome.

"Krista tried to appeal to their better natures," she told him. "She gave them every chance to be friends. Now we have to make sure the principal follows through."

His eyes met hers. "We?" he questioned.

"I'll go with you to talk to him if the situation doesn't improve. Krista is my responsibility, too."

She grinned suddenly. "I'm not above using the clout of my office to get a point across."

He liked the determined sparkle in her eyes as she mentioned using the influence of her position for the child. He liked the fact that she sided with him, aligning her concerns with his. As if they were a couple.

The latter notion brought him back to earth with a jolt. There was a physical attraction between them, but that's all it was. She'd made that clear. What woman would want a future with a gimpy vet who had three kids to see through college and ran a salvage yard for a living?

He ignored the obvious answer to that. "I appreciate your help on this. Trying to be a parent—"

Damn. He hadn't meant to bring that up.

"Is hard," she finished for him. "I know. We do the best we can, then we have to let go."

She took a deep, shaky breath, her bosom rising and falling with the emotion she felt.

"Sounds as if you've done a lot of thinking this past week," he said sympathetically.

She nodded. "It wasn't until I told my mother that I was quitting school and getting married that she told me about her marriage. She didn't want me to make the same mistake. I didn't want Zia to ruin her life. So we ended up perpetuating the errors of the past."

"How do you stop it?" he asked, not seeing a way past the mistakes.

"I think as parents we're honor bound to point out

the problems as we see them, but we can't force our solutions onto our children. We give them our blessings and our emotional support. If they need help, we let them know honestly what we can afford to do, but in the end, their problems are of their own creating and they have to solve them." Her throat moved as she swallowed. "So this is the great wisdom I'm trying to follow."

"Good thinking," he said softly, "but I don't think it will keep you from worrying."

"No, but it *might* keep me from making things worse." Her tone was more than a little rueful.

They smiled at each other. He felt a lightness enter his heart, as if they'd passed some great milestone along the road of life. "I'll try to remember this conversation. It should help me when Krista gets old enough to start dating. Maybe I'll live through it."

They finished the dinner in a thoughtful but more relaxed aura. The cherry cobbler and ice cream was one of the best treats he'd ever had.

Except for her.

He quickly pushed the notion far to the back of his mind. That was the best he could do since he couldn't dispel it completely. The wine caused a pleasant buzz in his head while desire hummed a counter-melody in his body.

However, as they finished the meal, their glances met more and more. One hunger was met, but another was growing. At last their eyes met and neither could look away.

"I don't know why I thought we could have a simple meal without complications, without…this," she murmured, a sweep of her hand implying all the passion that lay just beneath the surface of civility between them.

Since his mouth was too dry to speak, he stood and went to her. Rising, she faced him, her lovely face still and waiting. He waited, too, not sure where they were headed.

"I want to touch you," he said, unable to hide the huskiness or longing in the words. "How comfortable are you with that?"

Her smile was wry, shaky, endearing. "Very. I want kisses, but I'm not sure…maybe we should go slowly?"

"I can handle that. We don't have to rush." He took one step. Laying his hands on her shoulders, he drew her close so he could embrace her. "One day at a time."

"Or put another way—one kiss at a time?"

"Something like that," he agreed.

She settled against him as if they'd been created for each other. Unlike the half-finished statue back in his workshop, whose curves were so like hers in his mind, she was warm and pliable and, best of all, *real.*

As their lips met, his heart set up a cacophony of drumbeats in his chest. The pounding echoed in his head.

Caileen pulled away. "What is that?"

Jeff looked toward the door. A man's face, never before seen but strikingly familiar, peered back at him through the glass panels in the top half of the wood.

"I think we have company," he said.

Caileen's eyes went wide. "Brendon!"

She went to the door and flicked on the outside lights. The romantic ambiance disappeared.

"Come in. What are you doing here?" She peered out into the night. "Did you drive?"

"Hello, babe," the man said with an easy smile.

He had blue eyes and curly blond hair just like Zia's. He was tall, tanned and muscular. "Handsome as sin" came to Jeff's mind.

"Sorry to barge in," he said.

Jeff could tell by the amusement in the man's eyes that he wasn't sorry in the least.

"Why are you here?" Caileen demanded.

"I decided that since my weekend didn't work out, I would come up here. I think we need to hold a family conference."

"Oh," she said. "Zia isn't here."

"Well, I thought as parents we should talk first, then we can put out the word with her friends that I'm in town and need to make contact. Maybe that'll bring her around."

"I see." Caileen glanced around, saw him and seemed startled to find him still there. "Jeff, this is Zia's father. Brendon, Jeff is a f-friend."

Jeff noted the little stumble in describing him. He

shook hands with the surfer who could have still passed for twenty-five, maybe thirty. "Glad to meet you," he said. He turned to Caileen. "Look, you two have things to discuss, so I'll move along. We can talk later."

She nodded. "Yes. Thank you."

For what, he wondered. Leaving?

He said good night and hit the road, but not before noticing the very expensive sporty car driven by her ex-husband. The condo business must be going strong.

Erasing the rancid thoughts from his mind, he drove home. The house was silent when he entered. He checked on Krista and Tony. The two youngest members of the household were in bed and asleep. Jeremy's door was open and his room was empty. Jeff tried not to worry as he prepared for bed.

At two in the morning, Jeff was awakened by lights coming up the driveway. He rose and dressed in a pair of sweats, then pulled on heavy socks while his nephew parked close to the path. He and a companion walked through the swirling ground fog. Jeff met them at the door.

He sucked in a shocked breath at the identity of the newcomer. He managed a smile when the pair entered the house, bringing the scent of wet earth with them.

"Hello, Zia. Glad to see you," he said with more kindness than enthusiasm. The girl looked beat.

"Really?" she asked with a cynical weariness unusual for one her age. Emotion rippled over her face, and she seemed contrite. "I'm sorry to barge in on you like this."

"I insisted," Jeremy said.

The couple exchanged glances that caused a chill of dread to run along Jeff's nerves. It spoke of the shared intimacy of secrets, and that worried him in ways he couldn't define.

"Have you two eaten lately?" he asked, noticing that Jeremy looked as pale and drawn as the girl.

Jeremy nodded. "Yeah. We stopped on the way home."

"Good." Jeff leveled a direct gaze at Zia. "Have you called your mother?"

"Not yet." She again glanced at Jeremy, this time with a panicky expression.

"Could we wait on that?" Jeremy asked.

Jeff considered the hour. "I suppose it wouldn't hurt to sleep on it. By the way, your father is in town. He was at your mom's place earlier in the evening."

The girl blinked. She seemed about to sway, but Jeremy put an arm around her shoulders. "I thought Zia could have my room. I'll take the sofa," he volunteered.

"Fine," Jeff said with false heartiness.

After seeing the two younger people settled, he returned to his room. He glanced at the phone, but refrained from calling Caileen. He'd given his word to wait until morning.

And then all hell was going to break loose, he decided with fatalistic calm.

Chapter Twelve

Caileen stared out the window. Sunday, and Zia still hadn't shown up. Giving in to despair, she'd again called the girl's usual friends. All had sworn they hadn't seen Zia that week. Caileen had had no choice but to believe them.

She and Brendon had talked at length last night. Both of them had called their parents but to no avail. Zia hadn't gone to either set. By now their daughter could be anywhere.

She and Brendon had agreed they wanted Zia to finish her education, but if she chose not to, then she was on her own as an adult.

Tough love. Sometimes that was what it took. Caileen had advised more than one set of parents to practice that very thing. People made decisions; they had to live with the consequences without mom and dad bailing them out.

But it was nerve-wracking for the parents.

Her former husband was still asleep in Zia's room. She, on the other hand, had been up since dawn. Every emotion under the sun rippled through her with every passing hour. When the phone rang, she glared at the instrument and hesitated to answer, so sure she was of disappointment.

On the fourth ring, she picked it up. "Hello."

"Hey, this is Jeff. I have some news."

Her heart raced as soon as she recognized his voice. Now it went into cardiac arrest. "What?"

"Zia is over here."

She couldn't breathe, think, say anything. "Is she all right?" she finally managed.

"As far as I can tell. She's still asleep. All the kids are. I don't know whether I was supposed to call you or not, but I decided it was only fair to ease your worry."

"Yes, thank you." The words seemed inane. She tried to sort through the questions that hurtled through her mind. "When did she arrive?"

"Early in the morning. She called Jeremy. He brought her here."

"I see."

That was a lie. She didn't understand anything—why Zia had stayed away all week, why she called Jeff's nephew, why she was at their house and not her own.

The unpredictable tears burned Caileen's eyes and nose. She swallowed the lump in her throat and tried to think of practical matters.

"When they get up, I'll make sure someone calls and fills you in. Okay?" he asked.

"Is she sleeping with him?"

"Good God, no!" She heard him take a breath before he said, "Sorry. I should have explained. Zia is in Jeremy's room. He's on the sofa."

"Oh." She paused. "If Zia doesn't want to talk to me, tell her her father is here. She needs to speak to him."

"I mentioned that when they came in. Wait a minute," he said.

She heard another voice in the background and realized it was Jeremy's.

Jeff came back on the line. "Jeremy says Zia was at the campground out by the old road where the kids go to drag race. She was staying in one of the cabins they rent out during the summer."

"I never thought of looking there," Caileen admitted.

"None of us did." He hesitated. "I'll bring her home when she's ready. Or I'll call if…"

"If she doesn't want to come," she ended the sentence for him. "Thanks for your help."

"No problem," he assured her.

She couldn't decide how she felt after they hung up. To have the weight of the world suddenly removed from her shoulders sent her spirits soaring up to the ceiling. To know her daughter hadn't wanted to come home brought her speedily down to earth. However, at nineteen she hadn't wanted to face her parents and admit she'd been wrong.

Going to the bathroom, she showered and dressed. Since it was the weekend and she didn't have to go to work, she chose jeans, a green T-shirt and a flannel shirt in green and gold plaid.

After blow-drying her hair, she debated waking Brendon. However, until Zia appeared, there was nothing to do but wait.

She returned to the kitchen and poured another cup of coffee. Waiting, she decided, was not her strong suit.

Silence dominated the breakfast table at the Aquilon household. Krista stared at their guest as if Zia were a princess who'd deigned to visit. Tony ate with the dedicated attention of a starving teenager, never looking up from his stack of waffles and four slices of bacon.

Jeff's eyes met Jeremy's. They both looked at their guest. Zia ate one waffle, moving with the precision of a surgeon doing microsurgery. She was obviously drawing out the meal to prolong the time before the questions started.

Well, she was going to be surprised. Jeff didn't have any questions for her. He figured that was her parents' prerogative. She owned her explanations to them, not him.

After he finished, he stored the dishes in the dishwasher and returned to the table with a fresh cup of coffee. Seeing that the younger kids were through, he suggested they see about weeding the flower beds.

Tony and Krista took care of their dishes and went outside wearing their gardening gloves.

Zia put her fork down and met his eyes with a bravado that touched him. He'd seen the same look in the eyes of young soldiers when faced with their first battle.

"Did you sleep okay?" he asked.

She mulled the question over as if looking for a hidden land mine. "Yes. Thank you."

"Uncle Jeff," Jeremy said, breaking in hurriedly. "Would it be okay if she stayed with us for a few days?"

The request brought Jeff up short. He'd assumed her being here meant she was ready to go back home. Childlike, she'd wanted someone else to prepare the way, which was what he'd done by calling Caileen that morning.

However, he had to admit she didn't look young and irresponsible today. She appeared older than her years, old enough to be a sister to her youthful father.

Jeff stopped that line of thinking. Last night, taking off the prosthetic foot before getting into bed, he'd compared his circumstances to those of the surfer king, as he called the man in his own mind.

Caileen's ex was in excellent physical condition,

he was handsome as a movie star and he evidently had money. He was also interested in his ex-wife.

Jeff hadn't missed the flash of competitive spirit in the man's eyes, although his smile had been friendly—and totally self-assured—when they'd been introduced.

Several expletives dashed through his mind. He wondered where the ex-husband had slept last night, in the daughter's room or with the lovely counselor—

"That's okay," Zia said in a strained voice. "I can…I can find another place. I have friends—"

"Sorry," Jeff said. "I was thinking. Of course you can stay with us until you're, uh, more settled." He didn't have a clue as to what he meant by that.

Jeremy visibly relaxed. "I told her it wouldn't be a problem. She can take my room. I'll sleep on the sofa or in Tony's spare bed."

"I won't take your room," Zia stated flatly.

"Krista has twin beds in her room. You can stay with her." He managed a genuine smile and hoped the room-sharing wouldn't be a problem with Family Services. "Maybe you can give her some helpful advice about girl things."

For a second, he thought he'd said something wrong as tears filled their guest's eyes. "I won't stay long," she promised in a low tone. "Just until… until I decide what to do."

"Good," Jeremy said as if all were settled.

Jeff felt a tug of affection for the young man. His

nephew was always one to champion those in need. Not a bad trait, he admitted, but one that could lead to more trouble than one wanted to deal with.

"What about your parents?" he said. "I think you need to give them a call. They've been worried about you."

"I'll call now," Zia said.

"I don't think that's necessary," Jeremy told them. His gaze was trained on the front windows.

Jeff heard the purr of an engine and the crunch of tires on the gravel driveway.

Zia half rose, her pale face going a mottled red, then pale again.

Jeremy laid a hand on her arm. "We're here."

Jeff had a feeling that "we" included him.

Oh, hell.

Brendon drove too fast on the trip, but Caileen made no comment. She'd wanted to wait for Zia's call, but he had insisted they confront the girl and let her know what was what. She'd told him not to quarrel with Zia.

So instead, they'd ended up having a big fight at the breakfast table over how to handle the situation.

She pressed a hand over her right eye where the remnants of the migraine still lurked, a dark shadow of pain waiting to attack at a vulnerable moment.

How come life at forty wasn't more peaceful and settled than life at twenty? It didn't seem fair that she felt as unstrung now as she had then.

"Here we are," Brendon said, shutting off the motor.

"Don't shout."

"I'm not shouting."

"I mean, when you talk to Zia," she explained.

He got out of the car mumbling, "Maybe she needs some shouting at."

She couldn't argue with that. The sleepless nights, the constant headache, the overwhelming sense of failure churned like a geyser inside her. "Let's be calm. Okay?"

He gave a snort, then nodded. He had definitely awakened in a foul mood. She sighed just as the door opened.

"Hello," Jeff said in his deep baritone, the sound so normal, so soothing that she nearly rushed into his arms and burst into tears.

This was *not* the time. She concentrated on getting air into and out of her lungs while greetings were exchanged between the men.

"Come on in." Jeff held the door wide for them. "Zia is getting ready. She'll be here in a moment. This is my nephew, Jeremy," he said to Brendon. "Mr. Peters is Zia's father."

"Call me Brendon." He shook hands with Jeremy. "I understand you came to Zia's rescue last night. I appreciate that."

Caileen frowned at his man-to-man manner and easy charm with other people. He seemed to be able to flip a switch between fury and affability at will. By comparison, she felt mean and churlish in her anxiety over the meeting with Zia.

"Coffee?" Jeff asked, leading them to the table.

"Please," Brendon said, taking a seat as if he were perfectly at home.

She nodded and, seeing Jeff take his cup to the kitchen, went to help him. Their eyes met after he filled cups for the three of them. From the other room, they could hear Brendon and Jeremy talking. Jeremy was explaining about the campground where Zia had stayed that week.

"Did you get any sleep?" Jeff asked.

"Some," she said. "Not much," she added truthfully.

She glanced at the kitchen clock. A little before ten. She'd been up since six. Brendon's snoring in Zia's room had filled her with resentment until she reminded herself that their child was found and all was well. Sort of.

"I don't understand why Zia called your nephew," she continued. "It isn't as if they're friends."

She realized how awful that sounded and bit the inside of her cheek to stop the embarrassing words.

"They're classmates," Jeff said, pouring milk into a cream pitcher on a matching tray that held a sugar bowl. "Who knows what kids think?" he ended with a rueful shrug.

"I don't know what to do with her," she murmured so no one could overhear.

Jeff touched her shoulder. "Her father seems to have money. Maybe he could pay for her to stay at the university. She could share an apartment with some girls. That might be easier on everyone. Also, she needs a car of her own."

Caileen nodded. "That was one of the possibilities Brendon and I discussed last night."

"Talk it out now with Zia present. I never liked things presented to me as a done deal when I was a kid."

She thought this over. "Okay. Here goes."

His smile caused a sunny spot to glow in her heart. Feeling somewhat better, she picked up two cups and returned to the dining table with Jeff behind her carrying the service tray and his cup.

Zia came down the hallway. She stopped a few feet into the living room and looked from one parent to the other.

"Jeremy and I have things to do down at the shop," Jeff said. "Yell if you need anything."

After he and the young man left, Caileen observed them stop and speak to the two younger children before all of them headed for the workshop. They looked so comfortable together. By comparison, the tension in the house was thick enough to cut with the proverbial knife.

She took a seat at the table. Zia did, too, but without looking at either of them.

"Shall we call this family meeting to order?" Caileen asked, fighting the anger and recriminations that rose to her tongue.

Brendon glared at Zia. "I want to know what the hell you think you're doing?"

"Well," Caileen murmured, "that gets us off to a

good start." She studied their daughter. "Perhaps you could tell us what your plans are?"

"I don't have any," Zia admitted. Then she burst into tears, surprising them into silence.

"Tears aren't going to get you off the hook, not after what you put your mother and me through this week," Brendon informed her.

Caileen removed a tissue from her purse and handed it to Zia. If the tears were those of contrition, they weren't enough to erase the worry and fears of the past week, she realized. Zia was about to get a dose of tough love and reality.

"Your father is right. It's too late for tears. I'm angry and disappointed with your behavior. Running away was a childish thing, meant to punish *me* for your perceived wrongs."

Identical pairs of blue eyes stared at her.

"Everyone in this family is entitled to a life, including me," she continued, looking directly at her daughter, the words bubbling up from a deep pool of emotion accumulated during the past months of strife and anger and worry. "I lost sight of that."

"What about *my* life?" Zia asked, her tear-streaked face making her look vulnerable and woe-begone.

"I think that's what the last few months have been about. That's got to change. As long as you live in my house, you have to abide by the rules," Caileen said. "Otherwise you can move out and make your own rules."

Zia turned to her father as if in appeal.

He nodded. "Your mother and I are in total agreement. If you want to be treated as an adult, you act like an adult. You settle down and finish school and we'll continue to help you all we can. Otherwise you're on your own. It's up to you."

His manner was cool and controlled, one adult laying it on the line to another. Caileen was pleased at this show of solidarity. In the past, he'd always made her be the disciplinarian and he'd been the "fun" parent.

They exchanged a glance of mutual support and understanding. Her anger cooled, and for the first time in years, she felt they were united in their efforts concerning their child, that she wasn't alone in this.

Zia looked from one to the other. She gave a ragged sigh. "What do you want me to do?" she asked, wiping her eyes, then blowing her nose.

"Your father has some good ideas," Caileen said.

He gave her a quick, pleased smile, so handsome, so confident, so charming, it nearly took her breath away.

After outlining a plan for the girl to move to Oregon and go to the college there, he said he would pay tuition and rent for her to stay in university housing.

Caileen agreed to provide an allowance and food budget.

"If this doesn't fit with your plans," he finished, looking stern, "then you're on your own. If you agree, then you get our support for the three years you need to get your degree."

"What if I want to finish college here in Idaho?" Zia asked.

"Then I'll continue child support until you graduate or drop out, whichever comes first. In the meantime, you can earn your way this summer by working for me. My secretary is going out on maternity leave."

Together, she and Brendon laid out their ideas. The plan gave Zia some choices, but made the consequences clear if she didn't uphold her end of the deal.

"You don't have to worry," Zia murmured. "I'll do my part."

For a second, she looked defeated, her eyes devoid of spirit. Caileen experienced a motherly twinge of concern, then shook it off. When all was finished, she sighed in relief. For the first time in months, she faced the future with hopes for a happy ending. Sammy was out of the picture, Zia was staying in school, so all was well.

"Let's thank the Aquilons for use of their dining room for our conference and go home," she suggested.

"Life can get weird, can't it?" Jeremy said.

Jeff agreed. The two of them were working in the shop, Jeremy at the one-brick forge working on a blade for a new knife, while he tapped a scene of grazing bison, mountains in the background, into another blade using dots, the way Native Americans had formed petroglyphs in rock faces long ago.

His knife-making skills were becoming known in

Mountain Man Rendezvous circles and sought after by those who liked to collect such things. He prided himself on forming perfect edges and had taught classes in the ancient art at the local reservation college. Jeremy's skills were coming along, too.

He perused the copper sculpture that was almost finished. When it was delivered, the tycoon was going to give a big open-house party for his friends and local VIPs. He would have to go, too.

The reluctance within him to do so was stronger than usual. He didn't like gatherings where he was paraded as the "artist," and he didn't want to part with the figure.

There. That was the root of the problem. The statue would fit perfectly into a little bower of trees at the base of the backyard garden. With a bench for easy contemplation, a man could rest while he admired the work of his own hands. And thought of the woman who had inspired it.

Even better would be the woman sitting there beside him. He could stroke her warm flesh and compare her perfect curves with the imperfect ones that imitated them.

He thought of the family conference going on in his house. Caileen's former husband could certainly pose as a statue of Adonis or one of those Greek gods and heroes he had read about in school.

"Damn," he said as his hand jerked and he sliced across his index finger. He sucked the blood off and pressed his thumb to the spot to stop the bleeding.

"Cut your finger off?" Jeremy asked. It was the standard reminder between them to use caution.

"Not quite." He peered at the bison scene. At least he hadn't ruined the piece. "This is finished. See what you think."

Jeremy looked over the knife with an expert eye and tested the blade with his thumb. "What are you going to mount it in?"

"Bone. The scene continues on the handle with a buffalo jump and a stream. This is a commissioned piece, and the guy wants an elk at the stream. I haven't decided whether to put it in or not."

His nephew shrugged. "Too ornate for my tastes."

Jeff grunted in agreement. He fitted the blade into the carved-bone handle. The holes for the rivets were already drilled. He put the parts together and polished the metal to a gleaming finish.

Looking at his own reflection in the shiny surface, he saw a brooding face on a man with dark eyes and hair and nothing special to recommend him. He wasn't ugly, and he'd been told he had a great smile, but he knew he was just an average guy.

Nothing like the surfer king up at the house whose body was whole and perfect, whose looks were the kind to knock a woman off her feet. With the added attraction of once having been married, sharing worries over a child and knowing he was interested again, what woman could resist the temptation to see what might happen between them?

"They're leaving," Jeremy said.

"Who?" But Jeff already knew.

"The parents. Zia must still be inside the house."

Jeff had a sinking feeling in his gut. "Maybe we'd better go up and see what's happening."

In truth, he'd thought the girl would leave with them and they would all be one happy family again. His own little clan would be left in peace once more.

He and Jeremy walked up the path. Tony and Krista, who had returned to working in the garden, had finished weeding. The girl was tossing a softball with her brother. They watched him and Jeremy head for the house but said nothing.

Inside, Zia was still sitting at the table. Her eyes were red, but a smile was on her face.

"I wanted to thank you for coming to my rescue," she said to Jeremy. "And for putting me up for the night," she added, looking at Jeff.

"It was no problem," Jeremy said before Jeff could reply.

"My things are in your car. Would you mind giving me a lift home?" she asked. "School will be out at the end of next month. I'm going to work for my father this summer and see about enrolling in the university there."

Jeff wondered how Caileen felt about this decision. She would be alone.... Or would she be busy traveling back and forth to her ex-husband's place, spending the weekends there with him and their daughter?

Pushing thoughts of Caileen aside, he stayed busy

during the afternoon and finished the sculpture just as twilight darkened to nightfall.

By ten his left foot was giving him fits. Phantom pain. He was well-acquainted with it. He took some ibuprofen and dug out the mirror box from the closet.

The box was two feet wide and a couple of inches longer than his feet. A mirror divided the interior into a small space on the left and a larger one on the right. He removed the prosthetic foot and inserted both legs into the box.

The mirror hid the lower part of his left leg and reflected the image of his right foot, making it appear as if the left one was also in the box.

Using deep massage techniques taught by the military physical therapists, he rubbed his right foot while looking at the image in the mirror. The primitive part of his brain that thought the phantom foot was aching was fooled by the reflection. After twenty minutes, the pain had receded into the darkness that shrouded that part of his life.

He stored the box, turned out the light and went to bed. Another ache made itself known, one he'd tried to ignore all day.

Laying a hand on his chest, he listened to the harsh beat of his heart and remembered the long, lonely nights he'd lain in the hospital and known there wasn't a single person in the world who cared if he lived or died.

Odd, to feel that way again, especially when there

were three people sleeping in the house who did care, just as he cared for them.

The real reason surged up from his subconscious, forcing him to confront the truth. Zia was the spitting image of her father, a man who was whole and handsome. Throw in charming and wealthy. A woman would be a fool to want a disabled vet when she could have a surfer king.

Chapter Thirteen

Back at her house, Caileen put on a pot of fresh coffee, then stared into space while it brewed. Brendon sat at the table and looked over the Sunday paper. Glancing at the calendar, she realized this was the twenty-sixth of April.

The month was almost over and she hadn't any idea where the time had gone. Instead of a smooth flow, it had jumped from one crisis to the next.

She filled the cups still on the table and, with a heartfelt sigh, took her seat.

Brendon put the paper aside. "I thought things went well with Zia."

They exchanged parent-to-parent glances. Caileen smiled when he gave her a boyish grin that once would have turned her heart inside out. "You've become quite the resourceful parent," she complimented.

"I'm sorry I wasn't more help in the past," he said with unexpected earnestness. "It took me a long time to grow up." He paused, then said, "I'm wondering about us."

"Us?" she said, confused.

He gave her a slow perusal from eyes as blue as the Pacific on a perfect day. "You still knock my socks off," he said softly.

She was speechless.

"We've been through a lot together. I'm wondering if we should maybe give it another chance, see where things go. It would be good for our daughter," he added as a clincher.

Caileen focused her scattered thoughts. She studied her ex-husband, then stared into the steam rising from her cup.

Scenes from old memories glided past her mental vision—some happy, some sad, some fun, some lonely. All of them, she realized, were in the past.

And so was this man. Brendon, her laughing surfer hero, the love of her youth and the father of her child, now seemed like a childhood friend, one she would enjoy seeing at infrequent meetings, but not on a daily basis.

"I can see it's no-go," he murmured. "Is it the sculptor?"

She shook her head. "It's me. I think I need some time alone to discover who I am again."

He nodded as if he understood exactly what she meant. Now if only he would explain it to her, she thought, giving him a wry but grateful smile when he didn't argue.

"Then I'm off, babe. Tomorrow's a work day."

Outside, she walked him to the end of the patio. He stopped long enough to give her a very soft kiss of farewell. Somehow it seemed very sad, as if their paths might not cross again.

Long after he was out of sight, she stood there and rubbed a finger across her lips. Finally, noting the flush of green on the severely pruned shrubs, she realized life was returning, lush and verdant, to the plants.

A truck pulled up and stopped. Jeremy helped Zia bring in her books and few belongings she'd had with her. Caileen greeted them quietly, told them she was going for a walk and left them to their task.

At the end of the lane, she stopped and gazed into the meadow beyond the last house. Calves played in the grass while their mamas snoozed. Peace surrounded them.

Sucking in a deep breath, she envisioned new life flowing into her along with the warm spring air.

Caileen stared out the window at the clouds hovering over the mountains. She wondered idly if a storm was gathering and if it would bring rain to the valley. While they could use the moisture, she hoped it would be gone before the weekend. She wanted to hike and admire the wild flowers in the mountain meadows as she'd been doing for most of May, which had been a perfectly lovely month.

Today was Thursday. She and her best friend were having their weekly luncheon.

"Hey," Heather said. "Your gorgeous sculptor, foster father and personal friend just walked in. His picture was in the paper last Sunday. There's going to be an unveiling of his latest piece at the Chicago zillionaire's home this weekend. I heard the sculpture was commissioned for fifty thousand dollars. Are you going?"

It took Caileen a couple of seconds to follow that train of thought. "Hardly. I'm not in the zillionaire's circle," she told her friend, her gaze going to the man who stood beside the hostess's desk in the popular restaurant, his eyes searching the room, probably for the woman who handled his artwork.

"Are we expecting him?" Heather said with a hopeful leer. "Shall I wave him over?"

"No!" she said a little too forcefully.

In fact, Caileen hadn't seen Jeff but once in the four weeks since the impromptu conference at his dining table.

As Krista's counselor, she'd gone with him to a meeting with the school principal and had agreed to work with the girls who had bullied the orphan to see if they couldn't learn new methods of dealing with other children.

She'd also tried to turn the Aquilon case over to another counselor on ethical grounds.

Jeff had protested. The kids were comfortable with her, he'd said. They trusted her. That was the most important thing. So all was well as far as he was concerned.

Her boss had said if she could handle the situation, then she thought it was better if Caileen kept the Aquilon brother and sister under her auspices, given the caseload all of them were carrying these days.

So she'd gritted her teeth and continued with her work, her marriage classes and her life. Such as it was. She was still trying to "discover" herself or something like that.

"He's coming this way," Heather murmured.

Caileen felt her heart give a gigantic lurch, stop, then restart at a furious pace. Scientifically, she knew none of this actually happened; hearts didn't stop beating all of a sudden unless you died on the spot. But it felt as if all that had happened. And her pulse was racing.

"Hi," a deep baritone said.

She forced herself to smile, to look at him, to act as if all were completely normal. "Hi, yourself," she said casually. "You remember my friend, Heather?"

"Of course, the paralegal in juvenile court."

"That's right," Heather said, obviously surprised

and pleased that he'd remembered. She fluttered her darkened eyelashes at him, laughter in her gaze. "I saw your picture in the Sunday paper. Great write-up. How are things going for the famous sculptor?"

"Okay, I suppose. The city is interested in some stuff for a new park." He turned to Caileen. "I, uh, brought you an invitation for the open house. In case you're interested. It's for Saturday night."

Heather's eyes went wide. "At the zillionaire's little mountain retreat, all five thousand square feet of it?"

Caileen's heart lurched again when he smiled. He was just so…so…attractive and…and masculine and talented and thoughtful. "I don't know," she hedged, not sure what to say or whether she should see him.

Heather glanced at her watch and made exclamations about having to get back to work. "Here's for my share of the check," she said, tossing down some bills and hurrying out of the place like a rabbit with a hound on its heels.

A bubble of silence engulfed the table.

"Mind if I—"

"Please, have a seat—"

Caileen cleared her throat as they both spoke at the same time. He smiled and took the chair to her left. The hostess rushed over with a menu and water. The waitress took his order for a glass of iced tea and the steak special. The busboy cleared Heather's used dishes.

Jeff's dark gaze searched her eyes. She felt exposed and vulnerable, the way she'd been all spring, she admitted.

"Jeremy said Zia is with her father now. Are you okay with her decision?"

She nodded. "I think working for Brendon for the summer will be a good thing. He's found her an apartment to share with another girl, the daughter of his foreman. The girls will have to pay all their own expenses."

Jeff nodded. "A dose of reality. That should be a practical way of learning about the world."

"And a lesson she's needed to learn for a long time."

"I didn't say that." His tone was gentle.

The tears she'd refused to shed after her daughter packed and departed for Oregon—in the car her father had given her—fought with her self-control. She beat them back and won.

Her smile was genuine. "I'm glad Brendon is giving her this chance. I think she needs a change of scene. Going to the university in Portland will broaden her perspectives on life and people."

He nodded, hesitated, then asked, "Are you interested in going Saturday night? You can drive yourself," he added. "I mean, it isn't a date or anything. I just thought…actually the kids thought you might be interested."

When he pulled a white envelope from his shirt pocket and held it out, she accepted the invitation knowing she had no intention of attending the affair.

"It's cocktail casual, whatever that means," he told her, his broad shoulders moving in a slight shrug. "That's what Karen said to tell you."

"She's the interior designer, isn't she?" Caileen asked, tucking the envelope in her purse.

"Yes. She's decided to add original art to her business dealings and has asked to represent me on an exclusive basis. What do you think?"

He gazed at her in dead seriousness, which totally dissolved any thoughts she might have had, such as how compelling he was, how his hair gleamed in the filtered sunlight coming through the window, how she wanted to run her fingers through the lock that fell across his forehead.

"I think that's the way it's usually done," she finally said, suppressing the tumult he stirred in her. "But I'm not really familiar with such things."

"I probably should talk to Seth Dalton. He's an attorney up in Lost Valley. He might know."

"Yes." For the life of her, she couldn't think of another word to say. Her heart had slowed down, but its thumps were now so violent, she wondered if he could see how they shook her entire body. "Well, I have to go."

"Okay. See you."

She mumbled an incoherent reply, aware of his steady gaze on her back as she left. However, she was calm when she returned to her office and stored her purse, her mind oddly blank as if she couldn't think past the moment at hand.

The invitation in her purse seemed to send out faint vibrations, reminding her for the rest of the day and all of Friday that it was there, awaiting her decision.

She told herself a hundred times that there was no point in attending. Cocktails parties just weren't her thing. But she was curious about the sculpture. She'd seen it partly built. It would be interesting to see the finished work.

Jeff checked the crowd of faces, some of which were becoming familiar to him. He'd chatted with Taylor, the banker's daughter, for several minutes. She'd flirted with him, more out of habit than serious interest.

Karen, acting as his agent, had paraded him around and introduced him to the guests most likely to ask him to do something for them. Since he figured the money would come in handy for the kids' college funds, he'd made an effort to relax and "be natural but gracious," as she'd advised him.

He took a sip of the locally produced beer, nursing it along for the evening. Microbrews were the "in" thing, it seemed, along with local craftsmen, which was how he thought of himself.

After glancing over the crowd once more, he went outside without getting waylaid and stood in the roofed pavilion specially built for the sculpture he'd finished two weeks ago. A pang at no longer owning it struck him.

He took a deep, slow breath and walked around the female form as if looking for flaws, then came to an abrupt halt. "I didn't see you arrive," he said in surprise.

Caileen stood in the shadows, a wineglass in her hand. "You were talking to Taylor."

"You know her?"

"She's worked in her father's bank since she was old enough to reach the counter. I have my account there."

Her smile flashed white in the artfully concealed lighting that illuminated the sculpture. He joined her in the shadows.

She tilted her head toward the copper form. "What famous goddess or mortal is she?"

He hesitated, thought better of the impulsive reply that came to his tongue, then decided only the truth would do at this moment. He needed to know exactly where he stood with her. "You."

There was a wealth of meaning in the one word. He felt as vulnerable as he'd ever been in his life. Would she welcome this ceremonial laying of his heart at her feet? Or would she reject it?

Her hand jerked. She licked the drop of wine off her thumb and the edge of the glass.

Silence ensued, a lengthening strand of time that stretched and frayed into darkness.

"I realized when I started adding the curved pieces to indicate the shape of the body that I needed a perfect model for inspiration." He forced a laugh.

"She was around your height. You seemed the logical choice."

Standing beside her, he could smell her shampoo and the light perfume she wore. She was dressed in black slacks and top with a knee-length coat, also in black, that gave her a cosmopolitan air. The hair over her temples was pulled to the back of her head. She'd left a strand on each side to waft around her face. It was very attractive.

"I'm honored," she said.

He couldn't detect any emotion in her manner. The fierce, rapid heat of humiliation licked at his neck and face. "Well, I'm supposed to circulate," he said and turned too fast.

The toe of his prosthetic foot caught on a flagstone. Instead of making a smooth exit, he stumbled and fell right on her. His arms automatically closed around her while he got his bearings.

"Damn," he said. "Sorry about that."

"It's okay," she said in her usual gracious manner. Her eyes were filled with sympathy and kindness.

He managed to get himself off the patio and into the milling crowd inside the mansion without making a bigger fool of himself.

"Jeff, wait."

Ignoring her soft, anxious call, he headed for the exit as pain flooded his chest and circulated through his body. His phantom foot ached, making it difficult to walk without a pronounced limp. He made it to the door.

"Jeff, you aren't leaving?" Karen demanded, separating herself from a group and coming to him.

His answer was swift and determined. "Yes, I am. The dedication is over. I've been presented, I've mingled, now I'm going home."

She looked over her shoulder at the open patio doors, then back at him. "Drive carefully."

"Yeah. Good night." He headed for his truck.

Caileen laid a hand on the cool copper structure. She wasn't sure what she needed—advice from the silent feminine form telling her what to do?

You, Jeff had said. The sculpture was *her.*

She stared at each exquisitely formed curve, each line wrought with artistic perfection. She recalled his hands as he'd worked with the copper—so careful, so skillful, so…so *loving.*

You, he'd said.

Emotion rose from some secret well inside her, choking her, lashing at her, urging her to do something…to do it now…before it was too late.

With a stifled exclamation, she pushed her way through the crowd, her eyes darting left and right.

A gorgeous redhead planted herself in front of her. "He's gone home," she said.

Caileen tried to get past. "I have to talk to him."

"Why? To hurt him more?" The woman gave her a hard glare. "Leave him alone."

"I can't." She heard the words, felt the aching tumult inside her chest. "I can't," she said again, fierce now.

The other woman stepped aside. Frowning, Caileen rushed past her. Outside she saw the headlights of Jeff's pickup come on. She ran into the middle of the driveway and waited for him.

Jeff threw on the brakes as a woman materialized in front of the truck. He said all the curse words he knew. Nothing helped. He got out of the truck to find out what the hell she wanted.

"What?" he said.

His personal nemesis threw her arms around him. When he tried to free himself, he found he couldn't move. He was caught fast in the sweet feminine embrace.

"I was afraid I wouldn't experience this again," she murmured, her breath stroking his neck as she spoke.

He felt her lips follow her breath, leaving little kisses along his throat. He couldn't speak, couldn't breathe. "What the hell?" he finally demanded, trying to be cool, stern, to keep his distance, trying and miserably failing. How much torture was a man supposed to take, for God's sake?

"The statue," she said in a breathless way that threatened his heart and composure. "You said it was me." She drew back and gazed up at him. "Tell me what that means."

He managed a shrug and put his hands on her shoulders in a casual manner. Control, that was the key. He'd learned it countless times while learning to walk again.

"Jeff, please," she said.

"What does it mean?" he echoed, unable to hide the bitterness. "It means I poured every bit of skill I had into making her. It means I put my soul in every curve, every line as I shaped the metal. It means… hell, what does it matter?"

He tried to walk away, to get in his truck and drive off before he blabbed the whole, deep down, heartfelt agony of loving her…of wanting and not having. But she held on even tighter, her arms encircling him and clinging, her body pressed against his.

"What is this?" he muttered, trying to figure out what sort of compassionate, sorry-for-the-gimpy-guy act this was. Hell, she'd already rejected him….

"What do you want?" he asked, just to be sure, just to not get his hopes up or made any mistakes or anything.

"You," she said, laying those hot little kisses alongside his neck again.

"This is a dream." He snuggled her in a bit closer, not yet convinced he was hearing correctly, his brain so misty he couldn't think past the joy of holding her.

"Is it one that you want?"

"Yes," he said. "With all my heart."

They stared at each other for a long minute. Warmth spread through him as if a furnace had been lit inside him, but not from humiliation this time. Her eyes… There wasn't an ounce of pity in her beautiful eyes.

He smiled. She returned it.

"Let's go someplace," he demanded, turning them toward his truck.

"My car," she said, reminding him she'd come alone.

"I'll follow you to your place," he told her.

The trip took forever, but was too short. He had things he had to make clear to her. In the silence of her kitchen, he could hear the faint *whirr* of the clock. He had a sense of time passing.

"I'm forty-one," he said.

She nodded.

"You know about the kids, my home, how I make a living," he continued doggedly.

"Yes."

He scowled at her. "You aren't helping."

Her smile was tremulous. "I'm not sure what you're trying to say."

"Is there anything between you and your ex-husband?" He groaned at the harshness of the question, but he had to know the answer to that before anything else.

"Besides our daughter and some memories? No."

Her smile widened. Her expression changed, too, as a lambent glow filled her eyes. At least he thought it was lambent, or something like that.

"Jeff—"

"Caileen—"

He gestured for her to go first. She shook her head. He noticed her fingers were trembling. She was nervous, too. He could identify with that.

"I was attracted to you the first time we met," he told her. "It seemed mutual, especially later when we made love."

A rosy flush spread over her neck and face.

"You didn't seem repelled by my disability—"

"I'm not," she interrupted, her eyes fierce and flashing, a tigress defending her turf.

Caileen saw a flame leap into his eyes. She couldn't believe he'd been worried about her ex-husband or that he thought his injury might bother her.

He came to her then. "I'm not handling this very well. I've never asked a woman to marry me, so cut me some slack, will you?"

She smothered a laugh at the desperation in his tone. "All you want, but I think you can do better, maybe be a little more convincing that this is what you really want?"

"Yeah, the kids said I should practice."

"You talked to them about this, about us?" She found the idea amusing and somehow endearing.

"Yes. It would involve their lives, too. If you said yes."

Jeff knew he was making a sorry mess of proposing. Maybe he'd been too optimistic about her coming to the party.

"I was the one who ran after you and threw myself in front of your truck, then clung to you when you would have pulled away and left me standing there in the drive."

She gave a huff, drawing his gaze to her lovely

bosom. Her heat penetrated his shirt and blazer. Her scent filled his head and made him dizzy. His insides went all soft and buttery as yearning filled him.

"When I was working with the copper," he began slowly, "I found myself lingering over each piece, standing back to admire the lines as the figure took shape. I was more involved with it than any piece I'd ever done."

Caileen fixed her eyes on his. Wasn't he ever going to mention how he *felt?*

"About halfway done with it, I knew…"

He stopped and brushed the hair off his forehead with fingers that trembled ever so little. Something utterly feminine and unbearably sweet filled her.

"Knew what?" she asked. She laid a hand on his chest, sliding her fingers inside his jacket so she could feel the heat and strength of him.

His jaw clenched before he said in a very low voice, "I knew you were the one…the woman I loved."

The joy of hearing his declaration gave her an inkling of just how much she'd wanted it. It erased a hard ball of uncertainty inside her.

She pushed the lock of hair off his forehead and cupped his precious face between her hands. "I didn't know until this moment how much I needed to hear that from you. Since we met, I've found myself comparing other men to you. They all came up short."

"Even the surfer king?" His smile was wry.

"Even him. He's improved with age, but he doesn't hold a candle to you. I've watched you take responsibility and care for Tony and Krista and your nephew out of the goodness of your heart."

"Big deal," he scoffed.

"Yes, it is." Tears burned her eyes. "Oh, Jeff, how could I help but love you?" The tears spilled over.

He caught her against him in an embrace that said he would never let her go. "Thank God," he whispered. "I was afraid to believe it could happen." He kissed her softly, then lifted his head.

He touched the tear that escaped onto her eyelash. "Hey," he said softly, lovingly, "you remember what happens when you cry around me?"

She nodded. "Make love to me," she invited. "I want you. I love you."

He scooped her up, his muscles firm and steady as he held her close.

"I never thought I'd find someone like you, that happiness could be like this," he whispered. "We'll have a good life. I promise. You and me and the kids…the kids!"

"What?" she asked, startled as he set her on her feet.

"They're waiting for us. Oh, and we have to call Zia."

"Now?" she said blankly.

"Yeah. She and her father want to know how things are going."

"Brendon?"

Jeff grinned at the disbelief on her lovely face. "Yeah, Krista told Zia about this evening, so she and Brendon are waiting to hear how things turn out."

"This is bizarre," she muttered, not sure if she approved of an ex being in on the engagement announcement.

"I think we'd better get used to it," Jeff told her with a shrug of his broad shoulders. "He seems to think he's part of the family. Sort of."

Caileen couldn't help it. She started laughing. She knew life could take some weird turns, but this…this was ridiculous.

Jeff eyed her thoughtfully. "Are you okay with all this?"

She nodded, still laughing. "I'm fine." She snuggled in his arms. "Really, really fine as long as you're holding me."

"I plan to do that for a long time," he promised. "For all the years to come. Ready to go break the news?"

"Yes," she said. She remembered something she'd once read. *Happy families are all alike….*

No way. Each family was special and unique. She'd learned that over the years. But she liked the part about being happy…forever.

* * * * *

Don't miss UNDER THE WESTERN SKY,
the next book in Laurie Paige's new miniseries,
CANYON COUNTRY.
On sale September 2006, wherever Silhouette
Books are sold.